The Love of a Patient Man

The following story is a fiction. A product of the author's imagination.

ISBN-9798775663889

Cover art by SGerald

Contents

Coming soon

About the author

Acknowledgements

I would like to thank God. He kept pushing me to step out on faith and do what he had put into my heart. Thank you, R.F., for your encouraging words. To W. Williams for answering all my calls and giving me advice. To my mother and my son who believed in me. To my daughter who was a tremendous help, and to my Pomeranian, who was so patient during the writing process.

Chapter 1

So, I fell in love, did not see that happening. Because of a previous relationship that ended badly all I wanted was time to myself. I am not one of those people that just jump from one relationship to another. I got comfortable being on my own, and I was loving it. Then I met Fredrick Sanders. Trust me when I say I did not want to fall for him, but sometimes it is best to fall and get caught, because to fall and not get caught by the right one is not good. My name is Tasha Williams, and this is how it all happened for me. Have you ever seen someone and been drawn to them? I have found myself in this predicament. I am very attracted to this man. He is very handsome, caramel complexion, bald head, and muscles that you would want to reach out and touch. He has this smile that is so overwhelming to me. His brown eyes have just a hint of mischievousness about him that makes you wonder what kind of trouble we could get into together.

I was out walking one day, you know getting my exercise on and I saw him, he was running around the track. He was in great shape. I kept on walking, because it was a muggy day, and I wanted to hurry up and get it done. I was doing my stretches before I left, he came over and said hello.

He said that he wanted to let me know that he loved my hair. See, I had recently gone natural, and I let it grow out and changed the color. So, I said thank you, and I smiled at him.

He held out his hand and said, "I'm Fredrick."

I gave him my hand and introduced myself. He held my hand just a moment too long and gave me a great smile. There was something about that smile and it made me feel comfortable.

He asked if I came here a lot, and I told him I come as much as I can. He said he just started coming here, but he thinks he will start coming a lot more since he has seen something that has caught his eye.

I smiled and said, "Ok then. See you next time Mr. Fredrick." He said, "Likewise Ms. Tasha."

This day turned out to be better than I thought. So, I got in my car to head home, and of course the traffic is horrible. I am sweating like crazy, and all I want is my nice, cool condominium, and a very cold shower. My cellphone rings and I see that it is Alisha.

"Hi girl, what are you up to?" She asked me.

I tell her, I am just leaving my walking spot.

She asks if it was a good walk today, and I tell her, "It turned out to be great." I start telling her about Fredrick. By the time I am finished, she has us married and with a kid on the way.

She asked, "Did you get his number?

"No Alisha, I just met the man."

"What are you waiting for?" She asks. "You move too slow. I would have been all on that, girl." I started laughing because she really would have been on it, around it, and over it. The girl is man crazy.

"I am not like you, Alisha. I take my time."

"Alright, take your time, and watch that man get taken by the time you're ready." I think you have forgotten how this game is played, you snooze, you lose. You have been alone for too long, you need a man, girl. Have some fun once and a while. No one is saying marriage, but fun. "All you do is work."

7

"Alisha, calm down, I just met him, and at least my work makes me happy." I do not know how many times Alisha and I have had this conversation. She is always trying to set me up or push me on some guy. I finally tell her "I have to go." So, we hang up, but not before we make plans to meet up that weekend. All I know is that I must hurry home before Diva finds a place to handle her business. Diva is my furry baby, and I gave her that name because that is what she is, a diva. She was a gift from my last boyfriend. The boyfriend was a 'dog' too, and he had to go. I get to my condo. As I park my car, I see my neighbor, Ms. Nancy. Her place is about three condos down from mine. We waved at each other. Her husband passed away a long time ago so she is on her own, no kids, but she does have Buster, her furry baby. That is how we met she was walking her dog, and I was walking mine. We started talking and have been chatting it up ever since. Diva loves Buster, they have become the best of friends. I opened the door to the condo and Diva is right there at the door to greet me as usual. She was hopping up and down. I put the leash on her and back out the door I go. She finds a spot to relieve herself, thank God, because that means she did not go in the condo. I tell her, "Good girl" and she starts twirling around because she knows she is going to get a treat. I check on her food and water bowls, then off to the shower for me.

After my nice cool shower, I fix myself a green smoothie. While sipping on that, I am thinking about work for tomorrow. I work at a hair salon- I am a stylist, and I love what I do. I am always busy; Tomorrow I have a couple of men's haircuts, two highlights, and one color, along with two women's haircuts. As long as everyone is on time, I should be finished at five, and then I can get my walking done. That took my thoughts to Fredrick. What a smile. Then I remembered I better get my bag ready for tomorrow. Thank goodness for Ms. Nancy, she will come over around one and let Ms. Diva out then let her run around with Buster for a while. So, with my bag ready for work, I wanted to chill out with some tv time. One of my favorite things to do was pop some popcorn and watch some tv until I get sleepy. I like my quiet little world. Being alone does not bother me. Alisha was always saying, "Tasha, you are boring." I have no problem going out to eat or going to the movies by myself. If Alisha wasn't busy man hunting, we would hang out. So as far as I was concerned that was all the company I needed, and Ms. Diva of course.

My parents are no longer living. All I have is my brother, Austin. He is five years older than me, so at thirty he already seems to have his life figured out. A fantastic job working as a lawyer, married for two years now. Austin was happy and I was happy for him. We get together when we can. I started yawning so I thought I better take Diva out before bedtime. Diva jumped up and was at the door before I was. We have a great routine. I made sure no one else was outside before I opened the door, because I did not want Diva barking and having a fit. The coast was clear. So out we went. Diva really had to go. She found a spot fast. "Good girl, Diva." We ran back inside, and Diva got her treat for being good. "Time for night-night," Diva gets on her pillow. My last thought as I dozed off to sleep was a genuinely nice smile.

Chapter 2

When I get to work on Friday morning, as I was coming in through the backdoor, I can hear the same topic of conversation I always hear- men. It has been that way ever since I started working at Betty's Best Look Salon. You get to make your own hours, you supply your own products, and you pay to rent your booth. Ms. Betty is the owner. Everyone in the salon gets along, and that is hard when you work with a lot of ladies. There is a staff of six stylists, two shampoo girls, and one nail tech. Most of the ladies in the salon are single and feel like they know it all when it comes to dating. So, I try to stay out of their conversations about men. Keisha, the nail tech, just started seeing someone, and they were trying to tell her the four, one, one on all men. So, when Ms. Betty saw me, she said, "Tasha, what would you do if the guy you were seeing was always working late?"

"Oh no, guys, do not get me mixed up in this mess."

"Come on Tasha, don't you think something is up with that?" The other ladies are saying "Yes," and looking at me to respond. Keisha has a look of dread on her face. All I want to do is set up for my first client instead of participating in this conversation.

"Well?" Ms. Betty says, so I look at Keisha and say "I would get rid of him because something is up with that. Sorry, Keisha."

Then Ms. Betty and all the ladies start saying, "I told you so."

I feel bad for Keisha, she is so sweet, and we all know a little sweetness and a trusting nature, a man will take advantage of you. My first client walked through the door, and my day started. The conversation changed, thank goodness, and the day passed by fast. After work, I changed into my workout clothes, and started driving to the soccer field.

Looking for a parking spot, I noticed there was a lot of people out that day. Kids practicing, and some just running around having a fun time. Adults out walking around the field or running. I finally found a parking spot, I checked the time, Diva has been taken out by now and had her play date with Buster, so I have a little extra time before I must be home. I headed towards the track when I heard my name being called. I turned, and I saw the most gorgeous smile you would have ever loved to see. "You aren't going to start walking without stretching, are you?"

"Well, I guess I was, "I am just always in a hurry to get my walking done and most of the time I just hurt myself by stretching."

"Maybe I can help," Fredrick offered. "It is important to stretch before and after you walk. Come on we will stretch together. Tomorrow you will be able to tell a difference, and you will not hurt yourself, I promise." He held out his hand for me, and I put my hand in his. We found a quiet spot and he helped me with stretching. He asked, "How did that feel?" I told him, it felt great. I could tell he really did know what he was doing. He told me he hoped that he would run into me today. I blushed and said, "Really?"

"Yes," he replied. "Are you going to walk or run?"

"Walk," I said. "Do you mind if I walk with you?"

"No," I don't mind at all."

"Great, let's get started." We walked in silence, until he asked, "How has your week been?"

"It's been a good week. I am glad today is Friday though. How was yours?"

11

He said, "It's been busy, but good." Then he asked me, "What do you do for a living?"

"I'm a hairstylist," I replied.

"Ok, that explains it," says Fredrick.

"Explains what?" I asked.

"Your hair, it looks good, and I love it."

I say, "thank you." I guess I had a funny look on my face because he asked me, "What's that look for?"

I told him a lot of guys do not like the natural look. They like straight long hair. He said, "You will find out that I'm not like a lot of guys Ms. Tasha."

I had changed my hair and was really starting to love it. I let go of the perm and made my color a dark brown instead of black, then had some blonde highlights put in also. I felt so much freer and happier about the change. I keep a lot of curls in my hair now, it really makes the highlights stand out. People were always complimenting me on my hair. I told Fredrick it was much easier to take care of this way.

They were really walking at a good pace now. I asked him what he did for a living. He told me he was a trainer at a gym.

"I should have guessed. You just made me stretch everything on my body a while ago."

That is why he is in such good shape I said to myself. "So why are you out here instead of at the gym?"

"Sometimes, I just like to go outside and get some sunshine and fresh air. It also helps me relax. Plus, you get to meet people." Then there was that smile again. I thought to myself, did it get him whatever he wanted? I bet it did. "So, Tasha, how long have you been coming out here?"

I was still thinking about his smile when I noticed him looking at me funny. "I'm sorry, I was thinking about something. What did you say?"

So, he asked her again, "How long have you been coming out here?"

"I just started this summer. I pass by on my way to work, and even in the mornings there are a lot of people out here walking and I want to be out here with them instead of going to work. So, I thought to myself I should start taking my workout clothes to work with me and come out here before I go home."

"What will you do around daylight savings time?" Fredrick asked. "Do you ever think about going to the gym?"

"No," I don't like the gym scene. It is always too crowded, plus I have a treadmill at home, or I can get in an early morning walk around my subdivision. Sometimes my schedule allows me to do that. "I take it you come out here a lot?" I ask him.

"I do." he replied. "It's near the gym and not far from where I live. Tasha, I hope this question is not too personal, but I wanted to know if you were seeing anyone? Sorry, I just like to get straight to it."

Tasha looked at him with a nervous smile, then answered, "No," I'm not seeing anyone right now."

Fredrick did not realize it, but he had been holding his breath waiting for her answer. He let out a big breath of air when she said "No." He said, "I was hoping your answer would be no, because I would really like to see you again, and if I keep running into you here, I would not like you to think I'm stalking you."

Tasha smiled and said, "You are right, and I don't need a stalker." They both laughed. It was right at that moment, I realized

13

what time it was. I said, "Wow, we've been walking for a pretty long time, haven't we? I have to get home now."

Fredrick wasn't ready to say goodbye, so he said, "Not before some stretching Ms. Tasha. Remember what I said, before and after."

"Ok, just a few, though. I feel like I have a trainer now."

He said, "Do you need one, because that can be arranged." They both looked at each other and started smiling. He grabbed her hand and led her away from the track to stretch. Fredrick was telling me to concentrate and breathe, but I was busy trying to figure out how to answer his question about seeing him again. When he helped me up, he was holding my hand, and he did not let go. So, he said, "Will I get to see you again?"

Tasha looked into his eyes and said, "How about you give me your number, and I'll think about it." I pulled out my phone, and said, "Ok, what is the number?" I added his contact information and let him check to make sure it was correct. Then I told him thanks for all his help with the stretching lessons. I also let him know that I enjoyed walking with him. "I will give you a call, I promise."

"I look forward to hearing from you. Thanks for a great ending to my day."

Fredrick watched her walk away to her car. He did not know what it was about Tasha that had captured his heart, but he knew that he had to find out. That very first day he saw her, he just knew he wanted to get to know all about her. All that curly hair, those pretty brown eyes, and a complexion that radiated sunshine, with a body that showed she took exceptionally great care of herself. He could tell she was special. She had promised to call, he hope she was one to keep her promises. He could have spent the rest of the evening just walking with her. He wondered how come she was not seeing anyone, but then again, he was glad that she was not. Now all he had to do was wait for that call.

Chapter 3

On the way home all I could think about was Fredrick. I had to admit, he was a good-looking guy. Being a trainer, he was in great shape, and mercy, mercy that smile could just make you do things that would have you in church praying for forgiveness. He seems to me have me smiling and laughing a lot, which I love to do. In fact, I smiled all the way home. I was a little excited and a little nervous about Fredrick. I had told myself after my last relationship I would not be in a hurry for another one. After what Bryan had done to me, I had to be careful. I had thought that Bryan was the one, but he turned out to be someone I did not know. There was only one thing that I would be thankful for when it came to Bryan, he gave me Diva. Diva means everything to me. That is my baby. I could just sit at home with Diva all day long and be happy.

Home, sweet home, I thought as I unlock the door. I put down my bag, grab the leash and calm Diva down enough to get it on her. We head outside so Diva can handle her business. Just as we are about to head back in, I see Ms. Nancy heading out with Buster. Diva starts pulling me towards Buster, Ms. Nancy is also being pulled. We start laughing.

"How about these two?" I say to Ms. Nancy, "They act like they haven't seen each other all day."

Ms. Nancy starts shaking her head. She told me when she took Diva out, and how she took her over to her place so that the two dogs could have a playdate. "They ran around my place until they wore each other out, then they took a nap."

"Thank you so much, I don't know what I would do if I didn't have you helping me with Diva. She is so special to me, and I know you take loving care of her when she is with you."

Ms. Nancy says, "You are welcome, dear. I am only glad that Buster has a friend. You, Tasha, I think of you as the daughter I never had."

"That is so sweet Ms. Nancy." and I hug her. "Is there anything you need Ms. Nancy?"

She thought about it for a while, and then she said, "No, I think Buster and I are ok right now."

Sometimes I run little errands for her if she does not want to go out. It is the least I can do since she helps me with Diva. "Well, if you will excuse us, I have to get a shower now. I went walking after work. See you later!" I yell out to her and Buster. I get back inside, I made sure Diva had food and water in her bowls, then I head for the shower.

As soon as I stepped out of the shower, my brother calls. "Hi, Austin, how are you?" I say as soon as I pick up the phone.

"Hello, Tasha, I am good, how about you?"

"Good as can be, thanks for asking." Diva lets out a bark.

"Tell Diva hello." Austin says. We both laugh. "Just doing my big brother check." He tells me.

"Much appreciated, Austin, but all is well."

"Monica's birthday is coming up. I want to have a little get together and was wanting you to join us if you aren't busy."

"That sounds great. We all need to catch up anyway. We have all been so busy. Just text me the info. Will you be a plus one Tasha, or just lonely you?"

"Ha, Ha," I say, "That is so funny."

"Are you still not seeing anyone?"

17

Standing on the rug with a towel wrapped around myself, dripping water, I wanted to yell "No," but kept my cool, and said "No," I was getting tired of people making me feel like something was wrong with me because I was not in a relationship.

"Are you even trying?" My brother asked.

"I am busy, Austin, and I do not have time for the crap that comes along with dating."

"Not all guys are like Bryan, Tasha."

"I know, Austin. You are one of the good ones. Monica is a very blessed young lady."

"Thank you, sis, we both are blessed. I could not ask for a better person to share my life with. All right Tasha, I will let you get back to yourself." Austin starts laughing.

"You are full of jokes today, aren't you? Don't forget to send me the info."

"I won't, love you, Tasha."

"Love you back, Austin." I finally get dried off, lotion down and dressed. I say Diva's favorite words, "Let's go get Chick-fil-A." I grab my car keys, pick up Diva and off we go. Ms. Diva owns the car, she loves to ride. We get to the drive through, and it is the same as always. "Well, this is going to take a minute, this place is always crowded" I think to myself. "I think they put something in the food to keep people coming back. What do you think, Diva?" We get our order, and head back to the condo. I get comfortable on the couch, and Diva sits down waiting patiently for me to throw her one of her nuggets.

After we finish my phone beeps. I look at it, and it is Alisha. She is texting about us meeting up tomorrow. I text her back and say, "Yes, that will be fine, see you tomorrow."

Chapter 4

I slept late that Saturday morning. I had taken the day off. Saturdays are busy days at the salon, so I do not take off on busy days a lot. As I laid there that morning, I was glad I did. My phone started ringing, it was Alisha, "Morning, girl" Aisha said.

"Good morning," I reply.

"Are you still in bed?" Something told me to call you.

"Yes" I say, "I am having a great morning. I really needed this."

"You lazy cow, get up, and let's go have some lunch. How about Cinco's?"

"That is perfect," I say to her. "I love their salmon. How about we meet in two hours?"

"Ok, see you then."

I threw the covers back, grabbed something to throw on because Diva had to be taken care of first. Ten minutes later, I was getting myself together. I had on a maxi dress, with some wedges on, hair done, and little make-up on. I made sure Diva had everything she needed, and with that all done I grabbed my bag and keys and was on my way to meet Alisha.

We pulled into the parking lot at the same time, we waved at each other. Once we were out of our cars, we gave each other a hug.

"You look nice," I tell Alisha.

"Thank you, you know I try." Alisha is beautiful with her long dark straight hair down her back. Her mom is black, and her dad is white, and she has that mocha complexion. She is always up in the gym keeping fit. She says she must be ready for mister right. Alisha has on a little romper with a pair of heels that are to die for. We are heading inside the restaurant, and this guy is breaking his neck, checking us out, the sad thing about this is, he is with someone else. Alisha is looking at him like 'Really?' and then we burst out laughing.

We asked for a seat outside since it is such a lovely day. The server takes our orders, and we both get the salmon with veggies. Too early for drinking, so we get tea.

"So, what has been going on Alisha?"

"Not much, just working hard and trying to stay out of trouble."

"I know how hard that is for you girl."

Alisha works as an event planner. She is good at her job, and always busy.

"What are you working on right now?" I ask her.

"Helping this guy with a party for his wife. It is a surprise party. He said it is just because he wants to do something special for her. Can you believe it? He is that much in love with his wife. That is what I want Tasha, someone to love me just like that. Just because."

"That is what we all want," I say, "Just a little too sadly."

Alisha looks at me and starts to apologize. "I am so sorry; I didn't mean to bring up bad memories."

"It's ok, we're here to have an enjoyable time, so let us do that.

We are sitting there eating and laughing and having a wonderful time catching up. Alisha asks her, "How is that fine brother of yours?"

I smiled, "He is good, and still married."

"Well that just sucks for me," Alisha says.

I start telling Alisha how Austin is getting ready to have a small party for Monica.

"What? Do he need any help?"

"No, he's just doing something simple." Monica, himself, and he wants me to bring a guest with me.

"Well, are you?"

"Not that I know of."

"Come on Tasha, get back into the game. You have had enough time. I know Bryan did a number on you, but it is time. How about that guy from the track that you told me about?"

"I don't really know him that well, yet."

"Well get to know him."

"He did ask me out."

"Really?" Alisha was all excited about this bit of news. "When did this happen?"

"When I got to the track field on Friday, he was there, and he asked if he could walk with me. I said yes, so we walked, and we talked."

"That is great," Alisha says, about to jump out of her chair."

"I got ready to leave, he asked if he could see me again. I told him I would think about it and give him a call."

"That's good, so are you going to call him?"

I must have had a look on my face like I was considering it.

"Because Alisha said, come on Tasha just one date. Give him a chance. If it does not go well, you don't have to see him again."

"Ok, ok, I will have coffee with him. That way it doesn't seem like a date."

"Oh yeah, because a date would just suck," Alisha says with a smile on her face. I am so glad that you're going to do this."

"I will call him tomorrow."

"Great, I just want you to be happy."

"I am happy, living in my own little bubble, and here you are asking me to let someone in."

"You will be happy you did."

"We will see," I said nervously.

On the way home I stopped at Krispy Kreme and got donuts and coffee. I went home and got Diva, and we went over to Ms. Nancy's place. Ms. Nancy opened the door, she looked up and said, "Thank you God." She said she was just getting ready to make coffee.

"Well, I am right on time," as I hold up the donuts and coffee.

"Get in here girl," Ms. Nancy says, "We will sit at the table while Diva and Buster are running around like they have never met. So, what have you been up to already today?"

"Well, Alisha and I went out to lunch."

"Did you two have fun?"

"We did, we always do when we get together. Alisha is like the sister I never had. Like that older sister who knows what is best for you. Alisha is ready for me to start dating again."

"Really," Ms. Nancy says with a big smile on her face.

"Why are you smiling like that?"

"Because she is right, it is time honey. You know I love you, and I hope you will be ok with me telling you this, but you need to get back out there. You cannot keep to yourself forever. I am sure Ms. Diva is good company for you, but you need a two-legged person to make you over the moon happy."

I almost choked on my donut. After I recovered, I said, "That is what everyone has been telling me, but the thought of getting hurt again just makes me want to not get involved with anyone ever again."

"You are still young honey, not like me, get out there and live."
Then she gave me a hug.

"I am considering it, Ms. Nancy."

I went back home after my talk with Ms. Nancy. I had cleaning
to catch up on at my place. I could not stop thinking about my talk
with Alisha and then Ms. Nancy. I knew I could not keep to myself
forever, I just got comfortable and forgot about dating. I got the
laundry going, then dusting done, by then I had made up my mind to
call Fredrick. So, I got out my phone. Diva came and sat in front of
me, she looked at me as if to ask, 'Are you sure?' I looked at her,
and said, "No, I am not." I gave Diva a little rub on her head and
said a prayer as I made the call.

Fredrick picked up. My mouth went dry, and my heart started
pounding. I was so nervous. Fredrick had to say 'hello' again before
I said hello back.

"Hi, this is Tasha."

"Hello, Ms. Tasha, how are you today?"

"I am doing good today, how about you?"

"Well, that depends on you and if this is a yes call or a no call."

"You don't waste any time, do you?"

"I like to get right to it, so will I be having a good one?"

I just smiled because I loved his voice so much. It was deep,
and I could just see that smile of his on his face. "I am free
tomorrow; would you like to meet for coffee?"

"Yes," he says quickly. "You tell me where, and what time, and
I am there."

"I have to get some supplies for work. There is a Dunkin
Donuts near the beauty supply store. How about there?"

"Great, I like Dunkin," Fredrick says.

Would two o'clock work for you?

"That is perfect I do not have a client then, and even if I did, I would move them to a different time just to have some coffee with you.

It's just coffee, if tomorrow isn't good for you let me know, we can do this another time."

"Oh no, to you it might just be coffee, but to me it is so much more. Thank you, you have made my day, I cannot wait for tomorrow at two o' clock. Have a beautiful day, Tasha."

"Thanks, you too Fredrick. That went a little better than I thought it would I said out loud," Diva barked and did a twirl. "I take it that you are happy?" There was another bark. I smiled and told Diva she was way too smart. "Ok girl, we have about one more hour of daylight, how about a walk?" Diva ran to the door; she was ready to go. "We both need our exercise."

Chapter 5

I had a bad night; I did not sleep well at all. I could tell I had clamped down on my teeth all night, my jaw was hurting. I got Diva taken care of, then got myself a smoothie. I wanted coffee, but I knew I would be having some later with Fredrick. I got myself cleaned up and dressed. I kept my outfit quite simple; it was my day off and I wanted to be comfortable. My favorite pair of black jeans and a simple v neck t-shirt that had a loose fit, and a pair of black wedges. As I left, I told Diva to be good.

I got to the beauty supply store and got everything I needed. It was going to be a busy week at the salon for me and I wanted to be prepared. It is not good to run out of product when you are working on someone's hair, and I do not like to ask if I could borrow from another stylist. I got everything in my car and headed to Dunkin. I was driving and praying. You would think it was my first date ever, but wait, this is not a date, just a get together for coffee. I pulled into the parking lot, and there stood Fredrick standing near his truck, or so I assumed it was his, and crap he was looking good. As I was gathering my bag from the passenger seat, he started walking my way.

I was opening my door when he reached in and grabbed my hand to help me out of my car. "Thank you," I said.

"You are welcome," Fredrick said. We both said hello at the same time and laughed. "It is good to see you again."

"You as well," I said.

We started walking toward the door. Fredrick opened the door for me.

"You are a true gentleman, aren't you?"

"I try to be," he said. We found a seat. "So how do you like your coffee?"

"Oh, don't worry, I can get it."

As I starts to get up from my seat Fredrick puts his hand on mine and say, "I will get it, so please allow me," and smiles at me with that smile I just love.

So, I let him know I would like a medium coffee with cream and sugar.

"Any donuts or muffins?"

"Yes, please, a coffee cake muffin. Thank you."

"You are welcome," he says as he walks away.

I could not help myself. I had to watch him as he walked away. Then I smiled to myself. Not bad, I thought. He had a confident walk, his jeans were fitting just right, you could not do anything but look. "All right girl," I thought to myself, "You better watch it, or you are going to fall hard."

I was looking out the window when I heard, "I hope I am what you are thinking about?"

I couldn't do anything but blush because he was what I was thinking about.

Fredrick put my coffee and muffin in front of me. He put down his coffee and a couple of sour cream donuts. Tasha looked at what he put down and said, "Those are my favorite here at Dunkin."

"Really?" He said.

"Yes, I smiled at him. Now at Krispy Kreme my favorite is the plain glazed and the lemon filled. People like to say Dunkin is the best, but I tell them no way. There is no place that can beat Krispy Kreme in my opinion."

"You are serious about your donuts, aren't you?"

"Yes sir, I am."

"Well do not worry, I believe exactly what you just said. Krispy is better.

I held up my coffee cup and he held up his. We did a toast to Krispy and took a sip of our coffee. Then we laughed.

"You have a funny side, I like that."

"I love to laugh. Laughter heals whatever is bothering you. You could be having a bad day, but if you start laughing about something, you start to feel so much better."

"So, what else do you love Tasha?"

Tasha looked at Fredrick and smiled.

He would have sworn his heart skipped a beat. She was someone he just had to know and if possible, fall in love with. There was something pulling him to her.

"Well," said Tasha, "I love my job. When people come into the salon, they sit, we talk, you get to know them especially if they keep coming back. Sometimes you transform them into someone new. I love that look on their face when they see the finished look. They feel like a million bucks. They get a therapy session, because they sometimes come in with all kinds of problems and they just want someone to talk to, and instead of lying on a couch discussing your problems you sit in my chair, and we get to know each other.

"Do you cut guys hair also?"

"Yes, I have a suitable number of guys that come in too."

"How did you figure out that you wanted to do hair?"

"My Barbie dolls got me started, and then I had to learn how to do my own hair as I was growing up. I just knew I wanted to have my own salon one day."

"That is great" Fredrick said, and I could tell he really meant it.

"How about you? Do you love what you do?"

"As you already know, I work at a gym right now, but I want to start my own business. There are a lot of people who don't want to go to the gym, and they would love for me to come to their homes. They have a gym set up and would pay me very well to come to them. So, I am going to give it a shot, and see how it goes. Won't know until I try, right?"

"Yes, sometimes we just have to step out on faith and let God take it from there," Tasha says.

"You are right," Fredrick told her. "I don't tell people about what I want to do, because they want to try and talk you out of what you are trying to do. Or they are telling you that you will fail, so I have been keeping it to myself. Thanks for the words of encouragement."

"You are welcome, and I totally understand what you're saying."

"I just have a feeling that this is what I am supposed to do, and I am going for it." Fredrick leaned back in his chair and looked at her, "You know what you want don't you?"

"Yes," I said.

He smiled and looked into my eyes, and said, "I know what I want also."

I had a feeling that somehow the subject had changed when he said that. There was this look on his face that said I was what he wanted. I was not sure how to take that info. We continue to stare at each other for a few more seconds.

Fredrick broke the silence, "Tasha there is something about you that makes me want to know more about you. I am hoping that you will give me a chance to get to know you better. I don't want you to feel like I am putting any pressure on you, so why don't you think about it and just let me know."

I had to admit he wasn't too pushy; I was happy about that. "I will be at the track tomorrow after work, say about six o' clock. If you are free, you can come, and we could walk and talk some more."

He told me there was not anything that would keep him from being there. So, they started cleaning up their table, then they headed for the door. When they got to her car, Fredrick asked her what her plans were for the rest of the day?

I told him that I was going to drop my supplies off at the salon, then head home. I asked him if he had to go back to work?

He told me, "Yes, he had a client coming in for a session. Fredrick opened my car door for me. I got in and rolled down the window and said, "Thanks again for the coffee and donuts!"

"You are welcome. Be careful, and I will see you tomorrow."

"Ok," I told him.

Fredrick watched her car drive away and he thought to himself, "I am in trouble," because he knew, and felt it in his heart, Tasha was the one. He didn't know how this happened and he never thought it would happen to him. All Fredrick knew was she was different and incredibly special, and that is what he wanted.

I was looking into my rearview mirror; I could see Fredrick standing there watching me drive away. As much as I tried to fight what I was feeling for him, it was hard. It was as if he was a magnet, and I was just drawn to him, and it felt right.

29

Chapter 6

Tuesday was a busy day at the salon. My chair did not get cold all day long. Someone was always in it, keeping it warm. It was a good day, all my clients showed up, and they were on time. I was changing clothes getting ready for the track. All I wanted to do was get out on the track and start walking. Walking always clears my head and makes me feel better. So, I was going to enjoy my walk, and if he showed up, have some fun. Once I got to the track field, I saw how busy it was. It took a while, but I found a spot to park. I found an area to start my stretching, I wanted to make sure I did it right, so I took my time. I heard someone say, "Looking good." I turned around and it was Fredrick with that smile on his face.

"How long have you been there?" Tasha asked him.

"Long enough to see that you listened to what I told you about stretching."

"Of course, I listened," I said, "And plus, I had a great teacher."

"Thank you," Fredrick said. "So shall we get started?"

"Yes, I have been looking forward to this" Tasha said.

We had to say excuse me to some people as we started because it was busy, but we soon settled into a good rhythm of walking.

"So how was your day?"

"It was an exceptionally good day; I was busy. Everything went smoothly, and when you can say that working at a salon then you really had yourself a good day. Sometimes things can go very wrong."

"Well, I am so glad you had a good day."

"How was yours?"

"It was long, I could not wait for it to be over with so that I could see you."

I looked at him and smiled.

He told me about two new clients, and a few regular ones that he had that day. "So, to come out here and get some fresh air, and to be with you is helping me relax. How is the rest of your week looking, and do you work every day?" He was curious to know.

"We're not open on Sundays or Mondays, Tuesdays I am there, Wednesday I am there half a day, Thursdays, Fridays, and Saturday I work. I am in control of my schedule though.

"Ok, that is nice, it is sort of how it works for me also, and I like that I have control of my schedule. I can free myself up for other things that I would love to do instead he smiled."

Tasha swore if all you had to do was smile to make it to heaven, he wouldn't have a problem. I have a feeling that smile was going to be my undoing.

"So, what other workouts do you do besides walking? You are in great shape, and I know you do something else."

I told him how I love to do all kinds of cardio, and that I have a treadmill at home for those days the weather is too bad for me to be outside. "Sometimes I just put on music and do my own thing. My workouts depend on my mood, and what I want to do. I have my lazy days when I do not want to do anything but sit and watch television. When you are on your feet all the time it's hard."

"How do you do it?"

"A lot of soaking in the tub," Tasha laughed.

"You stand a good bit too," I said to Fredrick.

"Yes, trainers do, but when you love what you do it doesn't bother you."

"How did you get into being a trainer?"

"I played football in high school, so of course we were always lifting weights. After I graduated, I took some classes on being a professional trainer. It is so great to see someone transform their body. You get that person that is overweight, and they want to lose it and take better care of themselves. You get them to start eating healthy and working out, and you start to see changes with their bodies, and then their whole attitude changes. I love it when that happens."

"So, we both have jobs that we love," I tell him. "That makes us blessed."

"I guess we are," Fredrick told her. He jumps in front of her and started walking backwards so that he was facing her. "Do you realize that we have been walking for an hour?"

"Really? It doesn't seem like it."

He grabs me by the hand and say, "Time to stretch it out."

Once the stretching was done, they started walking to Tasha's car.

"This has been a long day. I am going home to relax," Fredrick says.

"Me too, this week has started with a bang, going to get cleaned up and get something to eat."

"I feel you," he said, "I am starving. And while we are talking about food, I think the next time we should get something to eat, you know, go out. How would you like that?" He asked, while looking into her eyes.

I was glad that he could not hear my heart beating, because I was nervous, this would make it a real date I thought to myself. "Ok, just give me a call and then we can figure out when and where."

"Great, I will call you very soon. Thanks for spending this time with me, this was fun."

I was amazed at how he thanked me for spending time with him. No other guy had ever done anything like that.

"Have a great rest of your evening," he says.

"You too Fredrick."

As he was opening her car door he told her, I love the way my name sounds on your lips."

Tasha was breathless, he was so close, and the way he was looking at me, I was speechless. Yes, it had been a while since anyone had made me feel like this.

He told her, "I will be thinking about you," he smiled and closed my door.

All I could do was watch as he walked away. A good minute had gone by when I realized someone was waiting on me to move so they could have my parking spot. I cranked up my car and headed for home.

Chapter 7

Once I was home, I made sure Diva was all set up, then I called and checked on Ms. Nancy. I took a shower and fixed myself a salad, then I hit the couch. Diva grabbed her favorite toy and went to her pillow. As I finished my salad I thought about Alisha. Ok, I said to myself, I better call her. We had not talked in a couple of days. I took my dish to the sink to clean it, then I poured myself a glass of wine. One glass would be ok I didn't have to be at work until ten. I pulled up Alisha's number, Alisha answered on the second ring.

"What is going on girl?"

"Nothing much, just wanted to touch base with you," Tasha told her.

"How about you with your busy self?"

Alisha told her she was just working hard and trying to play just as hard if you know what I mean, and they both started laughing.

"You do know you are a mess, right?"

"Well, one of us has to be, because you are not."

"I'll leave that to you," I said. Then I ask, "Anyone I know?"

"Well remember that party I was setting up for that guy who wanted a party for his wife "just because?"

"Yes, I remember, so how did it go?"

"It was good, the food especially, and the DJ was kicking it, and you know I had it decorated. Everything went great. I hooked up with this guy, he was like three of my favorite men all rolled into one. He had that deep voice like Mr. Vin Diesel, he was funny like

34

Will Smith, kept me laughing, and then he had the body of The Rock during his wresting days.

"Alisha you are so funny."

"Why, because I know what I want?

"Yes, and because you speak on it."

We are still getting together this weekend, right? How did your coffee get together go? Alisha asked Tasha.

"I have to say it went well. We talked, we laughed, and we got together today at the track."

"Really, Tasha that is good."

"He is very nice, and he wants to go out to eat next time."

"I am happy that you are starting to get back out there and have some fun."

"It is easy with Fredrick, he doesn't pressure me, he is the perfect gentlemen, and he listens to me when I talk."

"Are you sure he is real?" Alisha asked her.

"I know right?"

"I cannot wait to meet this nice guy."

"You forgot to tell me your hookups name."

"Micah, Mr. tall and dark she said with a dreamy look."

"This is amazing, and I love it, we are talking about men we are seeing."

"Calm down Alisha, you get too carried away. You may be serious, but I'm just going with the flow," I told her.

"Whatever Tasha, I know you and you're starting to melt."

"Melt, what do you mean?"

"That ice around your heart it starting to thaw out."

I took a sip of my wine and said, "Ok, Ms. know it all."

Diva went over to the door and gave me that 'I got to go' look. So, I told Alisha I had to go.

"Alright we will talk again soon," Alisha said.

"You bet, have a good night, Alisha."

"Sweet dreams Tasha!" You could hear her laughing as she hung up.

Once I got back in with Diva, I turned off the television and took my glass of wine to my room. As soon as I got myself set up in bed, and pulled out a magazine, my phone started ringing.

"Hello," I said.

"Hi, Tasha, I hope I am not disturbing you?"

I couldn't help but smile, "No you are not, I was just looking at a magazine."

"When I said I would call you soon, I bet you didn't think it would be this soon, but I wanted to hear your voice before I went to bed."

I did not know what to say to that.

"I also wanted to ask if your schedule for this week was full yet?"

"As of right now Saturday isn't all that busy."

"How about we go to dinner on Saturday?" he asked her.

"Ok, I would love too."

"Good I'll call you on Friday and we can talk about the details. Sweet dreams Tasha, I know mine will be."

"Goodnight, Fredrick."

I finished my glass of wine. Diva had hopped up and made herself comfortable at the foot of the bed. I turned off the lamp and snuggled in for the night. At first, I tossed and turned most of the night, then I drifted off and started dreaming. I sat up in bed and realized my heart was beating extremely fast. Diva was looking at me like 'what is up with you?' My fingers were touching my lips. In my dreams Fredrick was kissing me. It was a sweet dream because that brother could really kiss. I sat there until my heartbeat calmed down, then I looked at the clock. It was eight o' clock and I had to be at work at eleven. I decided I might as well get up; I was too nervous about going back to sleep. Fredrick might be there waiting for me in dreamland. So, I went and started talking care of Diva. It was going to be a rainy day, I noticed when I got Diva outside. So, it was going to be a workout inside day for me. I put in one of my cd's and got started with some cardio kick boxing. It was hard to concentrate, that kiss kept slipping back into my mind. I told myself it was just a kiss, get over it. Once I was finished with my workout, I took a shower. My stomach started growling, I was starving. I got the coffee going and then fixed myself a bowl of yogurt with fresh fruit. I ate that while waiting for my coffee. I checked my phone; Austin had sent me a text "Annie are you ok?" It was a little joke between me and my brother.

"Yes" I responded, "How about you?"

"All is well," he texted back.

"How is Monica doing?" I asked.

"Great, she is busy working."

"Tell her I said hello"

Austin told her, "Will do. I have decided to have the party at the house, and it will only be me, Monica, you, and whoever you bring. Her birthday is on Wednesday, I will remind you again soon."

"Ok, Austin." I sent him a kissy face emoji. I put down my phone and said, "All right Diva, I've got to get ready for work." I look through my closet as I drink my coffee. I wear a lot of black because that is what hairdressers do. So, today I grabbed a pair of black jeans, a black tank top, and black fashionable sneakers to complete my outfit. My day would not be long, but I did not want to be uncomfortable. I pulled my hair on top of my head and give

37

myself a look in the mirror. Satisfied with what I saw, I told Diva, "Time to go." Diva would spend the day with Ms. Nancy and Buster. So, I dropped her off Diva, and told Ms. Nancy I would bring salads back for us to have. Ms. Nancy told me, "That would be lovely."

Chapter 8

I got to work with fifteen minutes to spare, traffic was bad as usual. I get in, and it is quiet, something is wrong with that. I saw Ms. Betty was giving Keisha a hug and rubbing her back. One of the shampoo assistants, Maria, was working on Ms. Betty's client. Connie was at the desk checking out a client, but every so often she would look toward the back where Ms. Betty and Keisha were. When the client left, I went to the desk to ask her what was going on. If you want to know what is going on in a salon, ask the receptionist. Connie told me that Keisha finally got rid of her boyfriend, she found out that he was cheating on her. Connie told Tasha that Keisha came into work with tears in her eyes and Ms. Betty being the mom that she is got Keisha talking, and then the floodgates opened. The front door opened, and Tasha's first client came in.

"Hi Tasha!"

"Hello Michelle, how are you today?"

"Good" Michelle said.

"Come on over to my chair," I told her.

As I started my day things started to get back to normal in the salon. Keisha even got busy and was laughing a little. Four o' clock came, and my day was done. I went to the grocery store and picked up the fixing for a couple of salads. They steamed the salmon for me, and I took everything home and got it all set up, then headed over to Ms. Nancy's condo. I pressed the button for the doorbell, there was a lot of barking. The door opened, and there was more excitement. I gave Ms. Nancy a hug with one arm, and we headed to the kitchen area where she had a nice table for two set up. I asked her if the dogs needed to go out and she told me they were good. They had just come back in from a little walk about thirty minutes ago. I gives each of the dogs a rub, and then I headed to the sink to wash my hands. Ms. Nancy got out a couple of glasses and a pitcher of iced tea.

"I am so hungry," I tell her. I worked straight through lunch today, all I was able to eat was some fruit."

We sat down, and I passed her a plate.

"This looks great," Ms. Nancy told her. "Save some room because I baked some cookies."

"What kind?" I asked.

"Some peanut butter cookies. I know those are your favorite."

"Thanks! That is really sweet of you."

"No problem, I love to bake. How is your brother?"

"I talked to him this morning; he is doing good. He is going to have a little intimate birthday party for Monica in a couple of weeks. He is teasing me about bringing someone."

"Well, will you be going with someone?"

"I am not sure yet."

Ms. Nancy looked up from her salad. "That answer is better than a straight up no. You've been thinking about what we talked about last time haven't you?"

"Yes, what you said, what Alisha said, and what Austin has been teasing me about." I smiled.

"Good," Ms. Nancy says, as she puts her hand on mine.

"As a matter of fact, I will be going out to dinner on Saturday."

"That is great, I am so happy, and you deserve to be happy also Tasha."

"We will see how it goes on Saturday,"

"I will say a prayer," Ms. Nancy says with a smile and her fingers crossed.

"Thanks, I appreciate that, now where are those cookies?"

Ms. Nancy got the plate of cookies and put them on the table. I grabbed one, and bit into it.

"Mm, these are so delicious!"

Ms. Nancy smiled and said, "Thank you. Your salad was wonderful. These two" and she pointed at Diva and Buster, "kept me busy today." Thank goodness the rain let up and I was able to take them out for play time. That wore them out for a while."

Tasha was looking off into the distance smiling.

"Earth to Tasha," Ms. Nancy said, while waving both hands in the air. "What are you smiling about honey?"

"Oh, I was just thinking about something, I am so sorry."

"That is ok, I'm sure that whatever you were smiling about was more important than what I was talking about."

I started blushing because I was thinking about that kiss again. I grabbed a cookie and took a big bite; I didn't want to talk about the kiss.

"How about I pack you some of those cookies to take home?"

"That would be great," she said after she swallowed the cookie. Can I help you clean up or do anything for you?

"No, no, I am good, plus I like to keep busy."

"Ok, well I better get going, I have to get ready for tomorrow and get some rest." I gave Ms. Nancy a big hug and told her goodbye.

Fredrick was having a wonderful day. He had one thing on his mind and that was Saturday. He could not wait to spend some more time with Tasha. It was Wednesday and he had not seen her since Monday, and he had to make it to Saturday. To him that was a long time. Maybe hearing her voice would help him make it through the rest of the week. Once he made it through the traffic and got home, he threw his gym bag on the floor. He got out his phone and gave her a call.

Tasha answered her phone, and he was so happy. "Hello Tasha, are you free to talk?"

"Yes, how are you, Fredrick?"

He wanted to tell her he was floating on a cloud now that he was talking to her, but he said, "I am good, how about you?"

She told him she was good also.

"Tell me about your day?"

"Well, it was sort of a good day for me. A little drama at work, but it all ended well. I finished about four. Then I had lunch with a neighbor, and now I am home. Did you have a long day today?" I asked him.

"Yes, I had three clients at the gym and one home session. The home session took a while because he is a new client, and you must sit and talk and find out about that person. Then you tell them what you think will work for them. After that it is just a matter of them working hard and keeping account of it all."

They talk for about an hour and a half, he had only meant to talk for a couple of minutes, but once he heard her voice, he just could not stop himself.

"Tasha, just talking to you has made me the happiest. I am good and relaxed right now, and I might have to make this part of my nightly ritual.

"Anytime Fredrick, it was good talking to you too. Have a good night."

"You too Ms. Tasha."

The rest of the week went by fast. Fredrick called again on Thursday night and then again on Friday. He asked her if seven would be a good time for them to get together on Saturday? Tasha told him that will be fine with me.

"So do you want to meet, or would it be ok for me to pick you up?"

By now I was feeling comfortable with him, so I told him he could pick me up. "I will text you my address once you get here just text me and I will come out.

"Ok, I will see you tomorrow, Tasha."

"Goodnight, Fredrick." I was looking forward to tomorrow. I decided to give Alisha a call.

"Hi Tasha, what is going on?"

"That is what I am calling to ask you, Missy. You have been so busy; I am calling to check up on you."

"Well between work and Micah, I have been pretty busy. But a good kind of busy."

"I bet you have been. I won't keep you, just letting you know tomorrow is when Fredrick is taking me out."

"That is right, I almost forgot. Don't be nervous. Be your sweet self and have some fun, girl."

"I will, why don't you come over on Sunday and I can tell you all about it."

"That sounds like a plan, girl, and I will bring the wine."

"Great, goodnight, Alisha."

"Goodnight, Tasha."

Before I cut off my phone, I could hear a guy's voice in the background. I just started laughing and said, "that Alisha."

Chapter 9

Saturday was a breeze at work. I got in at nine, got my clients taken care of, and was out the door at three. I had plenty of time to get home, get walking time in with Diva, and then a hot bath. I made sure my nails and toes still looked good. Now came the task of finding something to wear. He didn't say where we were going so, I had to make sure that my outfit was good for anywhere we might go. I grabbed a little dress that looked like a v neck t shirt, it showed off all my curves, then I put on a pair of long hanging earrings and a nice bracelet too. I also got my favorite ring that looked great with anything. Next, I pulled out a pair of wedges that had straps that wrapped around the ankles. I was happy with what I put together. I really wanted to enjoy myself tonight. A look at the clock, and I realized that I better get moving before I was late. I sprayed on perfume, did a couple of turns in the mirror and thought perfect. Diva was looking at me with her head turned to the side like, "Where are you going?"

"Got a date little girl."

As soon as I pulled out a smaller bag for the evening, I got a text- "I am here."

"That's him," I told Diva. "You be good. I'll be back soon."

I got outside and saw Fredrick standing beside his truck. He was watching every step that I took. When I got in front of him, he smiled and told me how good I looked.

"Thanks, I wasn't sure how to dress since I had no idea where we were going."

He opened my door, held out his hand and helped me into the truck.

"You are dressed perfectly," he told me, then closed the door. Once he got in, he told me, "I hope you like Rays on the River."

"Yes, I do, I love to go there for Sunday brunch."

That made him happy because he was hoping she would like the restaurant he chose.

"I always eat too much at brunch when I go, then I feel miserable."

"I know what you mean," Fredrick said. "I think it's the layout of the food. It all just looks so good." We both start laughing.

Tasha started looking around his truck. "This is a nice truck." I noticed it was fully loaded. "Lexus has stepped up."

"Yes, they have."

We pulled up in front of the restaurant. Fredrick got out and gave his keys to the parking attendant. As he walked around to open my door, I noticed how nice he looked. He was wearing a royal blue shirt with a pair of black pants, and he smelled so good. There is nothing better than a good smelling man. His clothes fitted like they were tailor made just for him. I held out my hand and he helped me down. He held onto my hand as we walked inside. It just felt right.

He told the hostess, "Fredrick Sanders." As we were being taking to our table, Fredrick noticed other men checking Tasha out. He just kept his hand on the small of her back and smiled to himself. She was looking good. They got to their table, and he pulled out her chair.

I looked up at him as I sat down, and smiled, he was making me feel so special. I had to admit I was loving it.

The hostess let us know that our waitress would be with us soon, and she left.

45

"I am so happy that we are finally out like this. I have been looking forward to this evening. Even though this place is full of people all I see is you, Tasha."

I could not help but feel like a teenager and looking into his eyes I saw something that made me nervous. I saw a man that was into me whether I liked it or not.

The waitress came to take our orders. I broke eye contact and swallowed the lump in my throat. The waitress asked if we needed more time. We both said we were ready to order. I told her I will have the Salmon Oscar, and a glass of Pinot Noir. Fredrick ordered the Prime New York Strip and a glass of Cabernet Sauvignon.

"Great," said the waitress, "I will be back with your wine."

I was looking around, the restaurant was very full, the lights were low, and we were near the window. You could see the river. The atmosphere was great. I turned to see Fredrick watching me. I smiled, and he smiled back. Before I knew it, I said, "You have a really nice smile."

"Thanks, I like yours also."

Just as we were staring at each other, the waitress showed up with our drinks. We both reached for our glass and took a sip.

"So, how was your day?"

"It was good. Saturdays are always busy of course, but I was able to have a short day. Did you have a busy day?"

"Yes, I had three clients. I got in early, and I got out early. Do you have plans for tomorrow?"

"Yes," Tasha told him. "My friend and I are supposed to get together. She is going to come over to my place. Alisha is like the sister I never had. We have been friends since middle school. I have an older brother, and we are close. Do you have any siblings?"

"No, it's just me, I'm an only child."

The food was brought out, and it looked delicious. Once the waitress left, he told her that his parents made sure he had other kids to play with. He told her about his cousins.

"They felt bad that I was an only child. After they both had a few bites Fredrick asked, how is your food?"

"It is so good," I told him. "I hardly ate anything today so I could stuff myself with this food and I smiled. And yours?"

"As always, it is good."

We continue to talk and enjoy our food. We were having the best time. Our waitress came back to check on us. We both let her know that everything was good. Before we knew it, our plates were clean. Fredrick picked up his remaining glass of wine, leaned over and held his glass up for a toast.

"To a great meal, and company."

I picked up my glass and touched his lightly.

"Would you like some desert?"

"No," I replied, "I am stuffed."

"Are you sure?"

"Yes, thank you."

The waitress came back, and he asked for the bill. When the bill was taking care of, he asked Tasha if she was ready?

"Yes."

He got up and went to her chair as she began to stand, he took her hand in his as they were walking to leave. We saw the band playing, couples were on the dance floor, and a slow song was playing. He asked me if I would have one dance with him. I was a little hesitant because it was a slow song.

Fredrick whispered "Please," in my ear.

I nodded my head "Yes," because I did not trust myself to speak the word yes.

He led me to the dance floor. Once we got there, he looked at me, he could tell I was nervous. He told me, "I won't bite you."

I looked at him and smiled. I walked into his arms, then he said, "Unless you want me too." I started laughing. "Now that is better," he could feel me starting to relax. "Sorry, had to break the ice, and by me saying that I got you to relax a little. You were looking like I asked you for a kiss."

"I am sorry, I was a little nervous."

"Don't be, and don't worry, I will be asking for that kiss."

I looked up at him with my eyes very wide. He had that smile on his face that I am crazy about.

Fredrick loved the feel of Tasha in his arms. This was turning out to be a great night. He could tell the song was about to end, but he wasn't ready to let her go.

I had really relaxed and rested my head on his shoulder. When the music stopped, I lifted my head up.

He held my hand to his lips and kissed the back of it, and said, "Thanks for the dance, Tasha." I smiled and we both walked out.

We got back to my place, and I told him, why don't you come in if you have time? It's still early."

He said, "Ok," and pulled into a parking spot.

I turned to him and told him, "I hope you are a pet person. I have a pom."

"A what?"

"A Pomeranian."

"Oh, ok, I know what you're talking about. One of those little hairy barking dogs."

I hit him on the arm, "Don't talk about my Diva like that."

"Diva," he said.

"Yes, that is her name. Look, when we go in act like you don't see her because she is going to be barking when she sees you."

"I am good with pets; don't worry I know what to do."

We got to the door of my condo, I turned the key, and there was Diva. She was happy when she saw me, then she saw Fredrick, she started barking and ran towards him so that she could sniff him. Fredrick did what I told him and acted like Diva was not there. I told him to make himself comfortable. He headed for the small couch. By then Diva was just staring at him.

"Ok, she has calmed down. Can I get you a glass of wine?"

"That sounds great."

I went to the kitchen, and when I returned to the room Diva was standing by Fredrick and he was petting her.

"Well, you do have a way with the ladies, don't you?"

"Only certain ones," and we laughed.

I handed him his drink and sat down next to him on the couch.

He said, "This is a beautiful place you have."

"Thanks, I love it."

The couch they were sitting on was white with some throw pillows that were cream and gold. Two high back chairs also white with a gold pillow in each, there was a decent sized coffee table in-between the two chairs. The legs of the coffee table were gold with a glass top. There was a nice dish on it that was gold, and inside was scented red rose petals. A fur rug was under the coffee table. Diva and the rug were the same color, cream. There was a large flat screen tv on the wall. Behind the couch was a small dining table with four chairs, the same color as the rest of the furniture. On top of the table there were three gold candle sticks, and each was a different height. All the artwork complimented the room. This really was a woman's place.

"No kids hang out here, do they?"

"No, why do you ask?"

"It is so clean," he said with a smile.

"It's just been Diva and me. I've lived here for four years."

He looked over and saw some pictures. He got up and walked over to them. "So, are these your parents?"

I got up and walked over, "Yes," I said with sadness in my voice.

He looked at me. I proceeded to tell him about how I lost my parents in a car accident when I was twenty.

He said, "I am so sorry Tasha."

"Thank you," then I picked up another picture. "This is my brother, Austin. He is the best big brother ever. He is always there for me. Fredrick looked at her, she was back to smiling again. "How about your parents?"

"They're both still living. They have been married for thirty years and are still very much in love with each other. That is what I hope to have one day."

"My brother is married." They head back to the couch. "As a matter of fact, he is having a birthday dinner next week for his wife Monica. Would you please do me a favor and go with me? Austin has been teasing me so badly because I never take anyone with me when we all get together."

"I would be happy to accompany you."

"Great, it is next Wednesday at six thirty. It will just be Austin, Monica, you, and me. He just wanted something small and intimate."

"Sounds nice, thanks for inviting me. Now this bring me to a serious subject that I want us to talk about. I don't like to play games; I want to be upfront. I want to tell you how I feel."

I placed my hand over his and said, "I know." He looked at me. I told him, "I am feeling it too."

"Really?" He asked?

"I have to admit, I didn't want to, but I do."

He squeezed my hand and smiled.

"There is just one thing though, I need for this to go slow if you are ok with that then we can continue to see each other."

"I can do that," Fredrick told her.

Diva was watching them looking at each other, then she barked. They both looked at her and started laughing.

"Someone is feeling left out." I patted my lap and Diva hopped up onto it. After a few minutes of petting and playing with Diva, Fredrick told Tasha he was going to call her tomorrow to see about getting together. I said, "Ok."

He got up to leave and I told him they would walk him out because Diva needed to relieve herself since it had been a while. I grabbed the leash, and we headed outside. A spot was found quickly.

Fredrick walked me back to the door, "Thank you for a lovely evening," he kissed me on the cheek and turned to leave. "Until tomorrow Ms. Tasha."

Chapter 10

I got up with a smile on my face. I started my morning routine, then I called Ms. Nancy to see if she was going to church. She told me yes, so we decided to ride together.

When church was over, we stopped at the grocery store and picked up some things we both needed. I got back home with thirty minutes to spare before Alisha was due to come over. I had let Diva go over to visit Buster. I changed clothes quickly, then I set up a tray with grapes, cheese, and crackers. I pulled out the chicken wings I had picked up earlier and grabbed dip to go with them. The doorbell rung just as I finished setting up the glasses.

I opened the door and Alisha walked in pulling out a bottle of wine, saying, "Let's get to drinking, girl." We headed to the kitchen where there was an island with two tall stools. Everything was set up and ready. Alisha started pouring the wine, then we fixed ourselves a plate.

"Where is Diva?" Alisha asked her.

"She's at Ms. Nancy's."

"No interruptions, that is good. So, tell me how was your get together with Fredrick?"

"We had an enjoyable time; we went to Rays on the River. The food was great, Fredrick was good company, and the mood was even better."

"Girl, is that a smile I see on your face?"

"Yes, it is. I like hanging out with him."

Alisha's perfectly shaped brows lifted, "Do tell." She said.

"We came back here and had a glass of wine and talked some more."

"You let him in here?"

"I did," I said, as Alisha laughed at me.

"I only asked because you don't let anyone in. Did Diva like him?"

"Yes, they got along fine."

"Well, I guess he is in then."

"There is something about him. He makes me feel like I am special. I am so comfortable around him. I even asked him if he would like to go with me to dinner at Austin's next week."

"Ok, you are getting serious Tasha." She smiled and took a sip of her wine. "So, when do I get to meet him?"

"Soon, I promise. Just give me time to school him on you first, because you know, you be crazy."

"You know, I just keep it real. I have to, these guys think that they can just tell you anything and we are supposed to believe them. I am about to become a detective, girl."

"What are you talking about, Alisha?"

"Micah and I have been seeing each other for a while now, but something in my gut is saying wait for it. I have learned to trust my gut, so we will see what pops up. I am hoping my gut is wrong because I feel like he could be the one Tasha. He is a little of everything I have always wanted in a man."

"As ladies we are looking for that happily ever after, but in that happily ever after I need you to be trustworthy."

"Exactly," Alisha replied.

"How do we get that?" I asked.

"I guess we are going to have to keep kissing a lot of frogs until we get that prince we are searching for."

We were laughing so hard we barely heard the text to Alisha's phone.

"Ok, girl, got to go, that was Micah. He wants to get together."

"What happened to your gut feeling?"

"Well, I have to find out if I am right or not, don't I?" She said with a smile on her face. "So, until then, a girl can have some fun, can't she?"

"Like I was saying earlier, you are crazy, be careful."

"I will," Alisha said as she hugged me. After that she was out the door.

I started straightening up. Once that was all taken care of, I sat down to relax It was a little after five, I decided I better go get Diva. As I headed out, my phone started ringing. It was Fredrick. Tasha, what are you up to?"

"I was just headed over to get Diva, she it at my neighbors playing with her dog."

"What would you like to do?"

"How about we just hang out over here, it has been a busy week."

"Ok, how about I bring something over to eat?"

"That sounds perfect."

"Great, I have to wrap up a few things and I will be over around seven."

I went over to Ms. Nancy's. As soon as I rung the bell, I could hear dogs barking. Ms. Nancy opened the door, "You and Alisha finished early." I went inside and closed the door.

"Yes, her boyfriend texted her, and of course she went running. So, I thought I would come get my baby."

"Ms. Nancy started shaking her head and laughing, because even she knew how Alisha was.

"So, are you just going to relax for the rest of the evening?" Ms. Nancy asked me.

"Yes, and Fredrick is stopping by. He is going to bring some food."

"That sounds nice."

"He is very nice, and such a gentleman."

"That is very rare these days," Ms. Nancy said. "You will definitely have to bring him over some day."

"I will, I better go, I want to call Austin before Fredrick gets here."

"Please tell your brother that I said hello."

"I will, thanks for watching Diva."

"You are so welcome, honey. Have a blessed rest of your evening."

I gave her a hug, then me and Diva left. I pulled out my phone and called Austin. He answered by saying, "Annie, are you ok?"

I started smiling, "Yes, Annie, I am ok."

I was starting to think you forgot all about getting back to me about Wednesday or maybe you thought I assumed it would just be you and your lonely self."

"That is very funny Austin." He was laughing on the other end. "I called to tell you I have a plus one." I waited for his response.

"Really, Lil' sis?"

"That is right, I've met someone. His name is Fredrick. Just promise me you will not treat him like he's in court, Mr. Lawyer."

"Ok, but he better be a good guy."

"Trust me, he is."

"We will see sis."

"Do I need to bring anything?" I asked.

"No, just bring you and your guy. See you on Wednesday."

Sometimes my brother can be a little too protective. I hoped he would behave himself. My phone started to buzz, I checked it, it was Fredrick at the door. He was considerate enough not to ring the bell, which would make Diva start barking. I checked myself out in the mirror as I went to open the door. I unlocked the door and there was Fredrick holding a pizza.

"I hope you like pizza?"

"Are you kidding, of course I do, come on in."

He walked inside and paused to give me a hug, "It's good to see you."

"You too, let's go to the kitchen."

As we started walking Diva barked at him. He looked down and told her, "I am sorry, how are you Diva? You have that dog spoiled you know?"

I started laughing, "Yes, everyone tells me that." I started washing my hands. He waited for me to finish, then he washed his also. "I hope you like tea?"

"Sure, I do, this is Georgia, if you don't something is wrong with you."

"You couldn't have said anything truer." I grabbed a couple of plates and two glasses, then pulled the tea out of the fridge. "Ice?" I asked.

"He replied, "Yes, please." He watched her as she poured the tea. She had on a pair of lounge pants with a tank top that was long and loosely fitted, and under that she wore a strappy sports bra. Her hair was pulled on top of her head. She was beautiful he thought to himself.

We started eating the pizza. "Oh, this is good!" I told him.

"Good, I'm glad, I wasn't sure if you liked pizza or not, and I know you and your friend probably ate something, so I thought I should keep it lite. So how was your get together with your friend?"

"We had a fun time catching up, we had some snacks to nibble on, and some wine with lots of laughter. Her boyfriend texted her, and she took off. She is man crazy and does not understand how come I'm not. Sometimes I have to pull her back and sometimes, well all the time, she pushes at me to get out there."

"Well, I'm so happy you were out at the track that day. I was getting ready to leave, and I saw you. I must tell you; my heart skipped a beat when I saw you, and I knew I had to say something to you. I like hanging out with you, you have this goodness about you that is good for me. I know you want to go slow, but I am in love already Tasha." He reached for her hand, "Please know that I will do everything I can to make you happy. So now I am going to ask you something that I teased you about on our first date."

I was getting nervous because I knew what he was talking about.

"Can I kiss you? I have been wanting to do this since day one." He looked at my lips as he waited for me to answer.

"Yes," I told him.

His lips touched mine, and I could swear I was having that dream again because it felt the same as my dream. When we both pulled away, we were speechless. He rested his forehead against mine as we stopped to catch our breath. He told me, "I will never, for as long as I live forget this kiss."

"Neither will I." I said.

He reached over and gave me a hug, about two seconds later my phone started ringing. I got up to answer it. I said hello, but no one responded, so I said, "Hello" again. Still, no reply, so I hung up.

"Must be a wrong number," I said. "So, it's a pretty nice evening, how about we sit on the balcony and watch the sun go down?"

"I would love too," Fredrick told me.

They put the rest of the pizza away, grabbed their glasses of tea, and headed for the balcony. The set up was nice and simple, a couple of comfortable chairs with some pillows in them. There was a small table in between the chairs. Big green palm plants, and lanterns. There was also a colorful rug and drapes for privacy if needed. Diva even had a nice pillow to lay on. It was not a muggy day, but there was a ceiling fan to keep them cool if they needed it.

"I love it when I can come out here and relax," Tasha told Fredrick. I am truly a homebody, to me there is no place like home. I could be here for days and not go anywhere. I must be boring to you. Why don't we talk about you some?

"First of all, you could never bore me, and there isn't much for me to tell you. I pretty much keep to myself, I might kick it with the guys at the gym sometimes, but most of the time I am working. I just really want my business to take off. I picked up two more clients."

"That's great, sounds like business is moving right along for you!"

It is, so when I am free, I want to spend as much time as I can with you."

"Soon you are going to be so busy it will be hard for us to get together and enjoy evenings like this. Look at this sunset, isn't it just beautiful?"

"Yes, it is. See this is why I love to be with you. You help me relax, you encourage me, and you make me feel like a better person, so I will not get too busy for us, I promise. This is such a great spot you have here."

"When my parents passed away, I was so upset. Austin had me stay with him, I was with him for a year, then I started looking for a home of my own, and that is when I found this place. I had to talk Austin into letting me leave, he thought I needed more time, but I was ready to get out on my own. If he had his way I would still be there," She smiled. "Anyway, this is my home and I love it here. I have worked hard to buy everything in here. When I come home from work, I want to be able to relax. So, I fixed it just the way I wanted to. You work a lot; you are probably the same about your place-the relaxing I mean."

"Relaxing is hard for me sometimes. I have a loft, sure, I like it. I keep it as neat as I can, but I am a guy, so it is decorated like a guy lives there he smiled. Sometimes I feel like it is just a place for me to sleep at and then I'm up and gone again. I have got to stay on my hustle to get to where I want to be. If someone calls, I go and work. Word of mouth is everything in this business. I want this idea that I have to work out."

"It will Fredrick, just keep dreaming and have faith. Everything will work out. Don't be in such a hurry, all good things take some time."

"You are such a positive person. I love that about you."

"I refuse to be negative. God is good and has been good to me."

They talked for a while longer, had a bunch of laughs, then I asked if he wanted to go inside or if he was comfortable where we were? He said he was so relaxed, but how about we take Diva for a little walk so we can stretch our legs.

"Ok, it is about time for her to go out anyway."

We go and grab her leash and off we go holding hands. I asked if he had a busy schedule tomorrow?

"Well, the morning starts out busy and then there are a few at home appointments. I will be finished around four."

"That is great, how about I make you dinner?"

"Really," he stops and looks at me, "Seriously, can you cook?"

I look at him like "Really?" and we both start laughing. "I can, mister, I make a mean creamy chicken lasagna. You do eat lasagna, right?"

"Yes, I have never had that one before. I look forward to it."

"How about six thirty, and you bring the wine?"

"Yes, ma'am," he smiled.

That night as I was making my grocery list, I was smiling. I decided to make a lemon glazed pound cake also. I said to myself, "Can I cook? I will make him eat those words."

"It is crazy how bad you want something when you no longer have it." That is what he was thinking to himself, as he sat in his car outside of Tasha's condo. He knew he messed up, but he was going to do everything he could to get her back.

Chapter 11

I got back from the grocery store and started the cake. I wanted to get that out of the way first. Then I started getting the lasagna ready so all I would have to do is put it in the oven right before Fredrick was about due to come over. I made sure my place was looking spotless. I was feeling energetic, so I got on my treadmill. Afterwards, since I was already sweaty, I thought I might as well take Diva for a little walk, not far, just a walk around the condo. The cake was ready, so I took it out of the oven, then off Diva and I went.

After walking for ten minutes, I had a funny feeling someone was watching me. I stopped and started looking around, but I did not see anyone. I bent down, rubbed Diva, and said, "Let's go home, girl." I looked at the time and realized I had two hours to get ready. First, a shower, then I went back to the kitchen and made the glaze for the lemon pound cake. I put the lasagna in the oven to bake. Quickly, I made a salad also. "Okay, now to pick out something to wear." I pulled out a pair of black pleated shorts, I loved how those shorts looked on me and was hoping he would like them also. Then I got out a sleeveless satin top, for shoes my Michael Kors black and gold sandals. My shorts needed a belt, I remembered I have a thin gold belt. With that out of the way I started my hair and make-up.

A quick check on the lasagna, it needed some more time. I checked Diva's bowls to make sure she was good. On the way back to my bedroom I took a glance at myself in the mirror, I had a happy look on my face that said, "Yes girl, you are feeling this man." I shook my head to get out of the trance I was in. "Ok Tasha, get moving, he will be here soon. What fragrance should I wear?" I want something soft smelling. I settled on one of my Victoria Secret body sprays. Music, yes, I put on some slow jazz and started lighting up some candles. "Perfect," I said to myself. Then I took the lasagna out of the oven to cool off, it smelled so good. The pound cake had been glazed and was sitting on an ornate glass stand, ready to be enjoyed. I was ready. My phone buzzed, I looked at it, he was at the door. I liked that he was so considerate. I opened the door, "Hi, I smiled."

"Hello," he smiled back while walking through the door. He pulled me to him, while looking into my eyes he lifted my chin and kissed me on my lips. He held me and said, "that just wasn't enough" so this time he gave me a real kiss. It was slow and tender, then he just held on to me for a little while and told me he had been thinking about kissing me all day. He pulled back and looked at me, still holding one of my hands and said, "You look so beautiful, and you smell amazing."

"Thank you," I blushed, and we headed for the kitchen. He handed me the bottle of wine he bought, then he gave Diva a little rub.

"Wow, it smells great in here, and is that cake?"

"Thanks! And yes, it's my lemon glazed pound cake."

"It looks so delicious. We might have to do a workout after we eat," he said jokingly.

"I got in a good one before you got here, and I know you're always on your game."

"Can I do anything?" Fredrick asked.

"Sure, if you would please grab some glasses and that wine that you brought. You can get that wine opener, pour us some, and sit them on the table."

"Ok, I can do that," he says as he headed to the sink to wash his hands.

"Glasses are over there," I told him, as I grabbed the salad. I walked to the dining room table and put the salad down. Then I went back for the lasagna. I placed it on the table. He put the glasses of wine down, then pulled Tasha's chair out for her.

"Thank you, sir."

"No, thank you, I just know this is going to be delicious."

We started dishing out the salad, then the lasagna. Fredrick dug into the lasagna first. He closed his eyes as he chewed his food. He sounded like a kitten purring. I laughed at him.

"I have never had chicken lasagna before, and there's spinach in it, I take back my question."

"I put my hand under my chin, looked at him and said, "And what was your question?"

"You know, when I asked you if you could cook?" Tasha you can throw down," he picked up his glass of wine and said to the cook. I smiled and picked up my glass also. "Thank you for all of this," he was looking around at all the candles she had lit and hearing the music playing in the background. It made him happy that she did all this for him. "I really appreciate all of this."

"No problem, I liked doing it for you."

"Do you like the wine?" He asked her.

"Yes, it is very nice."

"I was thinking that we could take a bottle when we go to your brother's house of Wednesday."

"That is a good idea, I'm sure he and Monica would love it."

"You said your brother is a lawyer. What does Monica do?"

"She owns a little clothing boutique. Her clothes are unique. You will like her; she is sweet. Her and my brother are still in

63

honeymoon stage. I think it has been about two years since they got married. You will see what I mean when you meet them."

I stood up and started gathering the plates. Fredrick got up also and helped me take everything back to the kitchen. I started rinsing the dishes, I had the dishwasher door open. He put the dishes in, we had a rhythm going, like we had been living with each other.

"Thank you for your help."

"You are welcome. It's the least I could do."

"Do you have room for some cake?"

"You bet I do."

"Then let's cut this baby."

I put a slice in front of him. He took a bite. At first, he did not say anything, then after the second bite, he said," I think I am going to marry you, Tasha."

"Fredrick you're getting carried away. It's just cake."

"Yes, getting carried straight to heaven."

"You are hilarious"

"You can call me anything right now and I would agree." He reached over and cut another slice.

I was incredibly pleased with myself, I got him to take back what he said, and I could tell he was really enjoying himself. Diva jumped up and ran to the door frantically barking.

Fredrick looked at Tasha, "Is she alright?"

"She hears something." Tasha tried to calm her down, but Diva was not having it. "Something is up, she never gets this upset, the only time I've seen her like this is when," Tasha stopped what she was about to say and asked Fredrick if he could check outside and see if he sees anyone.

"Sure," he said with a worried look on his face. Lock the door when I go out. He could see she was not herself. She picked up Diva to calm herself. He went out, and she locked the door behind him. She just stood there leaning against the door rubbing Diva. About two minutes later Fredrick called her name from the other side of the door. She opened it to let him in and locked it back quickly.

"I didn't see anyone; I even checked the parking lot. Are you ok?"

"Yes, I will be."

He grabbed both of her arms and rubbed them he could feel the goose bumps on them. "Let's go sit down." He walked her to the couch and sat down. He pulled her close beside him. Diva hopped down, went to the door, and started sniffing. We watched her for a while. She finally stopped, went to her pillow, and laid down. They didn't say anything for a while, he wanted her to feel like she could talk about what happened when she felt like it. He could tell she was calming down, he asked if he could get her anything.

I told him I would love the glass of wine I left in the kitchen. He got it for me and his glass also. He handed it to me, I took a good sip and then sat it on the table.

"So, I know you were wondering what is going on, so here goes- I dated this guy named Bryan. He gave me Diva. She was the best thing to come out of that relationship. I broke up with him about a year ago, he was cheating on me. He got upset because I wouldn't give him another chance. He kept trying, it was like he was stalking me. Austin finally told him to stay away, or he was going to call the cops. Diva would get so upset when he showed up, that is why I am afraid it is him again. I heard he has turned to drugs now.

Fredrick listened to her the whole time without saying a word. He was holding her hand, he did not realize it but, he was squeezing her hand as she talked about Bryan.

"I am so sorry you had to go through that, so has it been a while since you've heard from him?"

"Yes, it has, but remember last night I got that phone call, and no one said anything. Well, I don't get calls like that. I am thinking it had to be him, I picked up my glass of wine again." I say, "Look, we were having such a wonderful time, let's not spoil it."

"Are you sure you are, ok?"

"Yes," I said. "I am just sorry you had to hear about my baggage."

"I will take you and your baggage if that is what I have to do," he smiled.

"I just love your smile; it is making me feel better. That smile is what got me."

"Oh really?"

"Yes, it says I am nice with a hint of mischievousness about me."

"I don't have a mischievous bone in my body."

"That is a shame then because that means you aren't any fun," I smiled at him.

"I am a lot of fun Ms. Tasha," and the look he gave me was very mischievous.

"I meant to tell your earlier you are looking so cute and that scent you are wearing is very nice." He began sniffing my neck, then my shoulder. I thought I would melt right there on the couch. Next thing I knew, we were kissing. He is holding me, and I was holding him. I was losing the battle with my mind; it was telling me to stop but I couldn't.

Fredrick was trying to remind himself to take it slow, but she was so intoxicating he could not pull away.

The doorbell rung, and Diva started barking. They pulled apart and looked at each other.

Let me get the door Fredrick said.

"Okay," I said with a worried expression on my face.

"Tasha you in there?"

"It's Ms. Nancy." I got it. I checked myself in the mirror before I opened the door. My lips were a little red but other than that I looked ok."

Fredrick stood up as I reached to open the door.

"Ms. Nancy are you ok?"

Buster ran in, heading straight to Diva.

"Yes honey, my lights are out. I think I might have blown a fuse or something," she said as she walked inside. Then she noticed Fredrick standing there. "Oh my, I have interrupted something. I am so sorry."

Fredrick said, "No ma'am, please come in."

Tasha closed the door. "Ms. Nancy this is the young man I was telling you about."

Fredrick looked at Tasha with a surprised look on his face and he held out his hand to Ms. Nancy. "Nice to meet you."

"Nice to meet you also young man."

Fredrick motioned for Ms. Nancy to have a seat. He asked her, "Did you call someone to take a look?"

"Yes, they said it could be a while, so I decided to come over here instead of being in the dark waiting on them to show up. I should have called first."

"No, Ms. Nancy, you did the right thing by coming over. Can I get you anything?" Tasha asked her.

"No honey, I am good. I just want them to hurry up, I have something coming on that I want to watch."

"How about I look for you? It could be something simple."

"Oh, that would be great. You sure you don't mind?"

"It would be my pleasure." Fredrick told her. "Let's go see what is going on."

I blew out the candles, then I grabbed the leash and hooked up Diva. When they got to Ms. Nancy's condo, she opened the door and reached for the flashlight, turned in on, and gave it to Fredrick.

"Ok, young man, the box is over there on the wall. You will see the panel."

"Ladies have a seat; I will see what I can do."

Ms. Nancy and I sat on the couch. The dogs were right beside us as we sat down.

Ms. Nancy said to Tasha, "I like him, and he is a good-looking guy. Is this a date Tasha?" She said with a smile on her face.

"I guess it is."

"Good for you, and about time, I am so happy that you are getting back out there."

"He is very nice, and I like being with him."

The lights came on, and the dog's started doing a dance. Ms. Nancy was praising God.

Fredrick came back into the room saying, "It was the breaker, sometimes that just happens. I guess you can call them and let them know not to come."

"Yes, I have to do that. I can't thank you enough!"

"You are so welcome."

"Now I want you two to go back to your date night before I interrupted you. Have a good evening young people. I have a show to watch and some ice cream calling my name."

Ms. Nancy gave Tasha a hug, as Tasha went to get Diva. Ms. Nancy told Fredrick, "She is a sweetie, be good to her. She means a lot to me."

He looked her in her eyes and told her, "I promise you I will."

Tasha came back with Diva, and ready to go. "Good night Ms. Nancy."

"Thanks again, Ms. Nancy said"

Before we headed back to the condo, we let Diva sniff around to handle her business. Once we got inside, I told Fredrick it was nice of him to help Ms. Nancy.

"It was no problem," he replied, "I am a little handy."

"She is very special to me."

"She said you mean a lot to her."

"We help each other."

The music was still playing so Fredrick pulled her into his arms.

"You love to dance, don't you?"

"Yes, as long as it's with you. I could hold you forever."

"In your arms is a delightful place to be," I smiled.

He gave me a twirl, and brought me back into his arms, then he dipped me.

"Alright, Fred Astaire."

He laughed, "Keep up Ginger."

We were in our own little world just having fun. We sat down to catch our breath.

"So back to work tomorrow?" He asked.

"Yes, my first client comes in around eleven. How about you?"

"My day will start at twelve, then I have some home sessions to go too. I guess I will see you on Wednesday when I pick you up. I will give you a call tomorrow night."

"Ok Fredrick, I really appreciate you understanding about how I want to go slow."

"Tasha, I completely understand from what you have told me so far, I get it. You will find that I am a very patient man. I will tell you this, Ms. Tasha, I am not going anywhere. Every time I lay eyes on you, I fall even deeper, so if you think because you want to go slow that I will not be down with that, then think again." He kissed me on the cheek. "Now can I pretty please get some of that lasagna to go?"

"Of course, you can, come on in to the kitchen, I'll fix you some and some more cake also."

I got him set up. As we walked to the door, he asked me if I would be all right?

"Yes, I don't have to go out for the rest of the night."

"If you need me just call." He gave me a hug and thanked me again for everything. Talk to you tomorrow night."

Looks like he is not spending the night. It might not be all that serious. I might still have a chance to get back with her. We did have something special, and I see she still has Diva.

Chapter 12

I got to work the next day, and everyone was looking at me and smiling. I wondered what was up with them. I had to get to my station and get ready for my client. There was a huge display of red roses there, I took the card out and it said, "Thanks again." It was signed "F." I smiled, "When did these come?" I asked Connie.

"About thirty minutes ago."

"So, Tasha what going on? Ms. Betty asked. "You got a new man?"

"If you are asking if I am seeing someone, then yes."

"Good for you I have been praying for you. You are too pretty to be by yourself, and you deserve happiness. Our girl Keisha is back in the game, isn't that right Keisha?"

"Yes," Keisha said, "This new guy, I have done my homework, he is the one.

"So, Tasha, how did you meet this guy?" Connie asked me.

"I was out walking at my usual spot, and we started talking, and have been talking ever since."

My first client walked in, and I was glad because I could tell they were going to drill me about Fredrick, and I was not ready to tell them anything. While my client was getting shampooed, I took a picture of myself with the roses and sent it to him. The caption read, "They are beautiful, thanks so much! What a pleasant surprise." I began working on my client. Two more showed up and I finished working on them, then I took a lunch break. I was sitting in the back room and my phone rung. I answered, at first no reply, so I said,

"Hello" again, then I heard, "Hello, Tasha." I was so shocked I almost dropped the phone; I knew that voice very well.

"What do you want Bryan?"

"No, how are you? No, I've missed you?"

"I will ask you one more time. What do you want?"

I heard him exhale on the other end, "Well that is an easy question for me to answer. I want you, Tasha."

"We are done Bryan, so please don't come near my place and don't call me again." Annoyed, I hung up the phone, then turned it off. I still had two more clients coming in, I did not want to be disturbed by him again. I returned to my station, just so I could see my flowers again and think of Fredrick. I leaned in and smelled the roses. The image of him smiling suddenly came to mind, and I couldn't help but smile at the thought of it.

I went to the front desk to look at my schedule for tomorrow. I had already marked myself out at three, so I wanted to see how early I needed to come in. I asked Connie if I could see tomorrow's appointments. My first client was at ten, that was going to be a highlight and a haircut. Then a guy's haircut, followed by a base color and blow dry. That was considered an easy day. I was working hard to save my money so I could one day open my own salon. It would be hard, but I was up for the challenge.

My next one showed up, and I was back at it again. I love what I do, and I had a great clientele. By the time I realized it, it was six and I was done and ready to go home. While getting my things together I remembered that I had turned off my phone. I saw that I had missed a call from Alisha, and a text from Fredrick. I texted him back and told him I would call him tonight. "Now, how am I going to make it home with these roses?"

I asked Connie to help me carry them to my car. On the way home I called Alisha back, but she did not answer, so I left a message- "Tag, you are it, call me when you can. We have to have a girl's session." That is what we called our talking it out time. When I got home Diva was waiting at the door as usual. There was a note from Ms. Betty letting me know Diva had been out an hour ago and she ate her food. I went to my room to put on something more comfortable so I could kick back and relax. As soon as I finished changing, my phone started ringing. I looked at it wondering if it was Bryan again, but it was Alisha.

"Girl, how are you?" Alisha asked.

"I am good, but I have a problem."

Alisha could hear it in her voice. "What is wrong? Do I need to come over?"

"No, I just need to talk about it. I have heard from Bryan."

"Girl, what? What does that scumbag want? Did you cuss him out and tell him to go straight to hell, because that is where he should be."

"Alisha, you need to calm down and breathe. You're more upset than me."

"That is because I saw how you were when things did not work out between you two, and plus, when you hurt, I hurt. Tell me, what did that jerk want?"

I told her about the call the other night when Fredrick was over, and about Diva acting crazy at the door, and the call today.

"I asked him what he wanted, and he said he wanted me. Can you believe that? After everything he put me through, I told him not to call me again."

"Girl, he is crazy. I can have him taken care of if you want me too. You know I know some people."

I didn't doubt that either. "Again, Alisha calm down. You should never call anyone crazy because crazy is you."

"I got your back girl, that is all I am saying." Alisha told her. "What are you going to do?"

"Nothing, I hope that this is the end of it."

"Are you going to tell Fredrick or Austin?"

"I will be talking to Fredrick tonight. He will be a little more levelheaded than Austin. Austin will try to pack me up and move me back in with him."

We laughed. "You're right," Alisha told her. "Look though if you need me to hang out there with you let me know. Don't underestimate Bryan, being on drugs will make you do some terrible things."

"I will be careful. How is Micah?"

"He is good, why don't we all get together? You know, a double date kind of thing?" Alisha said. "That way I get to meet your man, and you get to meet mine."

Tasha said, "That sounds great. I will talk to Fredrick and get back to you."

"Ok girl, love you."

"Love you back crazy."

I fixed myself some of the leftover lasagna and poured a glass of wine. The weather was starting to get cooler, so I went out on my balcony to enjoy it. I absolutely love my peacefulness. I finished my plate and set it on the table. Diva took that as her cue. She stood beside my chair and waited. I patted my lap, and Diva hopped into it. I started petting her. I was thinking my life was taking a turn that I didn't see coming. Sometimes things sneak up on you and Fredrick was a big sneak up. I was starting to wonder if he was home yet. I

74

did not want to bring him into my mess. I would wait and see if he brought up the subject of my phone being turned off earlier today.

It was starting to get late, and I still had to figure out what I was going to wear to the party tomorrow, so I took a shower. After that I looked through my closet for an outfit. I settled on a little black dress. One side was longer than the other and one shoulder had to be tied into a bow. I hung the dress on the door. The weather would be chilly that evening, so I decided to bring my black scarf that was sheer with a flowery design. I picked out a pair of black peep toe heels, and that completed my outfit. Tomorrow I would worry about jewelry.

It was time for Diva to go out one more time before bed. I grabbed my pepper spray and out we went. While Diva was sniffing out a spot, I kept looking around making sure we were safe. Diva did her business, and back inside we went. Once the door was locked, I made sure to set the alarm.

"Good girl! Let's go get your treat."

Diva grabbed her treat and off to the bedroom we went.

I pulled my hair up on top of my head and climbed into bed. I reached over to my nightstand and grabbed a magazine and started going through it. This would help pass the time until Fredrick called. As soon as I started reading it, my phone went to ringing. I could feel my heart racing as I reached for my phone. It was Fredrick. Relieved to see his name, my heart rate returned to normal, and I answered the phone.

"Hi Fredrick."

"Hello Tasha, are you good?"

"I am good."

"So, do you usually turn your phone off? I only asked because that way I'll be aware from now on." I was worried about you.

"No, I got a call, and I didn't want to be disturbed again, so I turned it off." I realized he wasn't saying anything. I thought I had lost the call, so I said, "Fredrick are you still there?"

"Yes, I am." His voice sounded different, "He called you, didn't he?"

I knew I had no choice but to tell him everything. "Yes, he called me."

"What did he say?"

"Fredrick, I don't want you to have to think or deal with my mess. I will take care of it."

"Tasha, I know you can take care of yourself, you have proven that, but now that we are in a relationship, and correct me if I'm wrong please. We are, aren't we?"

"Yes, we are."

"Then I want to make sure nothing happens to you. So, what did he say Tasha?"

"I asked him what he wanted, and he said he wanted me."

Fredrick had to calm himself down before he spoke again. "And what did you say?"

"I told him not to call me or come around my place again. Then I hung up."

"Has he called back since?"

"No, and I pray that he doesn't"

"You have to be careful. If he is still on drugs, you could be in danger, and that just does not sit well with me. Is your alarm set?"

"Yes."

"Did you already take Diva out for the night?"

"Yes. Fredrick, now if you don't mind, I would love to change the subject. I love the roses, thanks again!"

"Did you get them home?"

"Yes, they are scenting up my bedroom as we speak. I had a lot of questions thrown at me today at work about those roses and the person who sent them. One of my clients walked in, so I got off easy with my coworkers, but I'm sure they'll start asking questions again tomorrow."

"I take it you don't want to tell them anything."

"I don't believe they have the right to know all of my business. So, are you ready to meet Austin?"

"Yes, I am ready."

"He lives about thirty minutes from me, a really nice neighborhood in Kennesaw."

"Ok, I will get to your place around six, how about that?"

"That's good. I will be ready. We haven't gotten through this dinner yet, and we have been asked to go to another one already. Sorry, I really don't lead a busy life, but suddenly, I seem to be popular right now. I am really a working girl that comes home to her dog, and that was fine with me. Please say you can come to Alisha's with me. I said it's about time for her to meet you and for me to meet Micah."

"Yes, I'll go with you."

"It will be fun. You'll like her."

"I will like anyone you like."

"I hope you still say that after you meet Alisha, because I am telling you that girl is crazy, but she is a great friend."

"So, are you all tucked into bed?" He asked her.

"Yes, how about you?"

"Yes, I am in a hurry for tomorrow because I get to be with you. So as soon as we get off the phone I am going to sleep. That way when I wake up tomorrow, I will be closer to seeing you. Now,

I want you to get some sleep and hopefully you will dream of me. I know I'll be dreaming of you."

I had a feeling that he would be all I would dream of tonight. It was how he said it, his voice sounded all hypnotic as if he was casting a spell on me. I could just picture him smiling, it made me feel warm all over.

"I will see you tomorrow Ms. Tasha. Goodnight and sweet dreams"

"Goodnight, Fredrick."

Fredrick wanted to be there with her right now. He did not like that she was alone. He wanted to protect her.

....

"So, she thinks she can just blow me off like that," he said as he sat outside her condo. Today did not turn out how he wanted it too, but he would just wait for his chance and then he would make his move."

Chapter 13

I woke up startled, I could have sworn Fredrick was there with me. "Man, what a dream," I thought. I just knew it was real. I looked at the clock, it was time to get up and get started with my day. I realized I would have to get my coffee later, right now I needed a shower to wake myself up. I got ready in no time, got Diva taken care of, and I hit the door running. I would get coffee at work.

I got to my car, and there was Fredrick.

"Morning. I just wanted to be the first person you saw this morning, and to start your day off with,"- he reached into his truck and pulled out a cup of coffee and her favorite donuts. They were from Krispy Kreme.

I didn't know what to say about the sweet thing he had done for me, so I walked up to him and gave him a big hug and one of the hottest kisses he ever had. "Morning," I smiled up at him.

"I can bring you coffee and donuts every morning if that is the greeting I'll get."

"Thanks so much! I was just thinking I would get coffee at work. Aren't you supposed to be at work?"

"Yes, I had a little time before my next client was due." He opened my car door and said, "Now you can go off to work, I will see you later on this evening."

I got inside, buckled up, and started the engine. Rolled down my window and said to him, "I did dream about you last night," I smiled and pulled off waving.

He wanted to make sure she was ok, so he had to come and check. He could go back to work now and be at peace.

I got back home from work just when Ms. Nancy was about to drop Diva off at my condo.

"How was your day Honey?"

"It was good Ms. Nancy, how about yours?"

"Oh, you know, the usual, these two chasing each other, some barking, our walks outside and then a nap for all of us." She laughed. "You're home early today, what are you up to?"

"Austin is having that little dinner for Monica this evening."

"Oh, are you taking that nice young man?"

"Yes, Fredrick will be going with me."

"That is nice dear, I hope you have a good time. I will let you get ready. Diva might be ready to eat now, and she took care of her business already."

"Ok, thank you Ms. Nancy!" I took the leash, and Diva and I went inside thank goodness I will have enough time to get ready. I better hurry Diva, my prince will be here soon.

I heard my phone buzz. It was Fredrick texting to tell me, he was outside the door. I had just finished putting on my heels. I walked over to the door and opened it. Fredrick had his back to me looking out towards the parking lot, so when he turned around, he just stood there staring at me. I smiled and told him to come in.

"My, my, my, you are the best thing I have seen all day." He grabbed my hand, held it up and gave me a spin around while he stood there and checked me out. "Beautiful," he told me, "Just beautiful." Then he pulled me towards him and gave me the sweetest kiss you could imagine.

When the kiss was over, I looked at him and told him how very handsome he looked. He was wearing black pants, a black t-shirt, a black blazer with a pair of nice shoes. His only jewelry was an expensive looking watch. Of course, he smelled good. My hands were on his chest, I could feel his heartbeat. I looked into his eyes, and he was looking into mine.

"You have the prettiest eyes, I could just get lost in them, and I love your hair like this."

I had it swept over to the side. He was holding me like he did not want to let me go.

"Maybe we should get going before we start to have our own party," he told her while still looking deep into her eyes.

We had not pulled away yet, I said, "Yes, I think we'd better go." I grabbed my scarf and he draped it around my shoulders. Then I got my bag, he kneeled and petted Diva. She licked his hand. I also did the same, and then we they left.

Tasha was right, Fredrick thought to himself. Austin and Monica lived in a nice neighborhood.

"There is the house," I told him, and he pulled into the driveway.

"This is nice," Fredrick said, looking around.

"It's too much for me," I said. "I am happy with my little condo."

"Alright, here we go," he reached into the backseat and grabbed the bottle of wine. Got out and went around to open the door for Tasha. They walked up to the front door and Tasha rung the bell.

Austin opened the door, "Lil' sis, glad you could make it! Please come in."

"Hi, Austin!" She gave him a hug. "Austin, I would like for you to meet Fredrick. Fredrick, this is my brother Austin." They shook hands.

"Nice to meet you Fredrick," Austin said.

"I thought my sister was joking with me when she said she was bringing someone with her." Austin looked at Tasha and smiled. I smiled back and said, "He is real Austin."

Fredrick said, "It's nice to meet you also. Your sister speaks very highly of you."

"Really, because she treats me like I'm a big pain she wants to get rid of."

"You are a big pain Austin," Monica says as she approaches them standing in the doorway, "But that is what makes me love you." She gives him a kiss.

"Thank you honey, Monica this is Fredrick."

She reached out for a handshake, "Hi, it's nice to meet you."

"You also," Fredrick said as he was shaking her hand, "And Happy Birthday!"

"Thank you," then she turns to Tasha and says, "Hello sweetie. How are you?"

"Hi Monica, Happy Birthday, I am great, thanks for the invite, and we brought some wine for dinner." I turn to Fredrick, and he hands it over to Monica.

"Thank you, guys, so much, it will go great with dinner. Why don't you guys go to the living room, and I will go put this in an ice bucket to chill. Be right back."

Fredrick started relaxing a little. Her brother and his wife were warm and friendly. Tasha and her brother looked alike, you could see the resemblance and the closeness was obvious. Monica was a pretty, petite woman. Her and Austin made a lovely couple.

Heading to the living room Fredrick was taking it all in. There were hardwood floors, and the place was decorated like it was featured in a magazine. He must do very well as a lawyer because this place was amazing.

The living room had a bar. There was an exceptionally large flat screen television on the wall. It had panels that could slide over and cover up the tv if you wanted it hidden. There was a huge glass chandelier that hung in the middle of the room, and there was a big couch that looked like you could sink into it if you sat on it. Large pillows were on it with a huge fur throw also. A couple of chairs sat on the other side of the couch with high backs. The plants were so big and green one would think they were fake, but they were real.

"Please have a seat. Can I get anyone anything to drink?"

"I think I'll wait until we eat," Tasha said.

"I'll do the same," Fredrick said. "This is a very nice home you have."

"Thanks, we love it and hope to start filling it with kids."

Monica came back and headed straight to Austin. She made herself comfortable right on his lap, then he wrapped his arms around her.

Tasha looked at Fredrick and said, "What did I tell you? This is how it will be the whole night."

Fredrick smiled and picked up her hand and held on to it. She leaned into him and felt amazingly comfortable. They looked up and two sets of eyes were on them.

Austin asked, "How did you two meet?"

"We met at the track field that I go walking at, and we have been hanging out ever since," Tasha told him.

Fredrick told them, "I am a trainer at a gym that is close to the field, so sometimes I feel the need to go out and get some fresh air. It gives me a chance to think. I am trying to get a business going where I go to client's homes. I already have some clients; I'm just trying to expand."

"That is a good move because these days everybody is trying to get fit," Monica said as she stood up and told them, "We can head to the dining room now."

They all walked that way. The table was set up beautifully.

"Monica, this looks so pretty," Tasha told her. There were tall candles that were lit in every corner of the room.

"Austin had someone come and set it up and I didn't have to cook either." She smiled up at him as she sat down in her chair that he held out for her.

Monica was just turning thirty. "So how is thirty?" Tasha asked her sister-in-law.

Monica smiled and told her, "I don't feel any different now, but when I turn forty, I'm sure I'll feel a significant difference."

"No matter what age, you will still be my beautiful sexy wife."

"You are so sweet," and she blew Austin a kiss.

The server came out and greeted everyone. Then she began to put down their salads. The wine had already been poured. Austin picked up his glass, held it up, and said, "To my wife, happy birthday, I love you."

"Happy birthday," joined in Tasha and Fredrick, then everyone began eating their salads with the conversation flowing.

About twenty minutes later, the server came back out. She refilled glasses that were empty, then she took away their salad plates. The main course came out, "I hope you will like what is on the menu tonight," Austin said. "It's baked lobster tails, with lemon basil finger potatoes, and asparagus.

"It looks and smells amazing," Tasha said.

"Yes, it does. I can tell you right now I will love it," Fredrick said.

"Great!" Austin said, "Lets chow down."

Tasha asked Monica how business was?

"It is good. I have had to hire one more person to help in the store. We have even had some celebrities come through, so that has been great for my little store. Atlanta is a wonderful place to have a business, and Fredrick, you are going to be amazed at how well your business is going to do. You get a client that loves you, and just like that they will start telling others and you'll have so many people calling, making you wonder how am I going to handle this? I wish you much success with that," she lifted her glass and leaned it towards him.

"Thank you," Fredrick said. "Tasha's doing a fantastic job encouraging me," he looked at her and smiled.

The server came back out to refill drinks and take away plates. Fredrick put his hand over his glass and so did Monica. Fredrick asked Austin what made him decide to be a lawyer?

"I had a very good friend get locked up for something that wasn't his fault, and he couldn't afford a lawyer, so he got stuck with someone who did a poor job defending him, so that is why I became a lawyer."

The server returned holding a cake with the number thirty on it. She placed the cake and the knife on the table. She also put down some small plates, then left the room.

"That is a delicious looking cake," Tasha said.

"It's my favorite," Monica said, "Italian cream cake. My baby went above and beyond tonight." She got up, went over to Austin, and gave him a kiss, then she walked over to the cake.

Austin started singing 'Happy Birthday.' Tasha and Fredrick joined in.

"Thank you, guys, I couldn't have asked for a better birthday!" She put a slice of cake down in front of everyone. "I know it is my birthday, and I don't have to give a gift, but I have one." She held out her hand for Austin to join her. He walked over.

"What did you do?" He asked her.

She looked at him and smiled. "Dear husband, light of my life, I am pregnant."

"What?" He said with a big smile on his face. He picked her up and started going around in circles, then he thought about what he was doing and stopped. He put her down and said, "I am sorry, are you ok?"

"Yes," she said, "But please, no more spinning in circles."

"Congratulations!" Tasha told them. She looked at Fredrick and said, "I am going to be an auntie."

"Here baby, sit down please. When did you go to the doctor?"

"I started feeling funny about three weeks ago, so I made an appointment, and the doctor told me I was going to be a mom. So, in about eight months we will have a little bundle of joy. I hope you aren't upset that I kept it a secret, but I wanted to wait until my birthday to tell you."

"No, I am not upset. He picked up her hand and kissed it. You have made me the happiest man on earth." You could tell that they were truly in love with each other.

Monica said, "Please eat your cake."

"Speaking of eating, I haven't seen you with any morning sickness."

"Well, I haven't had any, I guess I'm one of those blessed and fortunate women that don't have it. The doctor said we," and she rubbed her stomach, "Are doing well."

"I want to go to the next appointment," Austin told her.

"I have one next week."

"Great," he said. "Do you like the cake?" he asked his sister and Fredrick. They both shook their heads because their mouths were full of cake. Once they swallowed, they both said, "Delicious." They looked at each other and smiled.

Austin could tell that Fredrick was a goner by the way he looked at his sister. He also thought, now would be the perfect time to get to know more about him. So, he said, "Ok ladies, I want to show Fredrick my gym and get some pointers on a few things. Would you please excuse us?"

"The *ladies* will go back to the living room and wait on you fellas," Monica told them.

As Monica and Tasha headed to the living room, Tasha asked her sister-in-law if that was wine, she was drinking earlier?

"No, I had the server pour me some cranberry juice to make it look like I was drinking wine. I had to keep Austin from questioning me." He is always a lawyer Monica smiled.

"I am so happy for you guys, and I can't wait to be an auntie."

They got to the living room and sat down.

"So, tell me about Fredrick, is this serious?"

"Well, he has told me it is for him, and I think I'm falling. He is a great person, it has been so easy for me to talk to him about anything, and he truly listens. I told him I wanted to go slow, and he agreed, he has been very respectful, and he treats me like I am the only woman in the world. How could I not fall for all that?"

Monica was watching Tasha as she spoke about Fredrick. She could see Tasha was already in love. You could just hear it in the way she said his name. Her sister-in-law was happy. Tasha was such a sweet person, and she deserved happiness.

Austin took Fredrick to his home gym. He wanted to be able to work out when he could and not worry about going to a gym. He wanted his own, he told Fredrick.

"This is a nice setup, and you have the latest equipment, so how often do you work out?"

Austin told him; he tries to get in about four days a week it just depends on his schedule at work.

"That is good," Fredrick responded.

Tell me, how serious are you and my sister?"

"I am so serious when it comes to Tasha, and I have told her that. I think because of her problems with her ex-boyfriend she is being cautious, and I can understand and respect that."

"So, she told you about Bryan?" Austin asked like he was shocked.

"Yes, she told me, and there is something I want to talk to you about." Fredrick told him everything that happened. Austin was not happy about what he heard.

"That guy hurt my sister so bad, but I can see she is better now, and I think that has something to do with you. She never brought him here, she knew I did not trust him, and she should not have either. The way you two look at each other and from what I have seen tonight, you two have a connection, and I like what I see. My little sister means a lot to me, and I will do anything to protect her. We will keep this to ourselves, but please keep me informed if anything else happens and I will slip you my card with my number on it before you leave.

Fredrick nodded his head.

"Let's hope he stays away because I will have him locked up if he doesn't. I know my sister; she would try to handle this all by herself."

"I know," said Fredrick.

"Maybe we should head back to the ladies before they come looking for us," Austin told him. "I am glad we had this talk; I will not let Tasha know what you told me."

"Appreciate that, I don't want her upset with me, but I think you should know what is going on."

Monica and Tasha were giggling about something when the guys got back into the room.

"What is so funny?" Austin asked them.

They looked at each other and said, "Nothing," then began giggling again.

The guys took a seat beside their ladies. Monica asked Austin if he learned any new workout tips?

"Yes, I did, don't worry, I will keep this body rock hard for you," and he gave her a squeeze.

"Meanwhile, I will get fat," Monica said pouting."

"Baby, I will help you, we are in this together."

Tasha cleared her throat to interrupt them. "We are going to call it a night, you guys have a lot to talk about and to celebrate, plus the little mother needs some rest. Thank you for letting us celebrate your birthday with you and for sharing the baby news.

"Yes, we had a wonderful time, and it was such a pleasure to meet you Fredrick said."

Austin stepped away and went to a drawer, pulled out a card with his number on it and slid it into his pocket. As they were walking to the entryway, he thanked them for coming. "Monica and I enjoyed meeting you, Fredrick."

"Thanks," Fredrick said. He gave Austin a handshake, and that is when Austin slipped the card into his hand. The ladies were hugging and did not notice anything.

"Congratulations again to the both of you, that is going to be one lucky baby," Fredrick said.

As Tasha hugged her brother he whispered in her ear. "I like him." She kissed his cheek and smiled at him. Fredrick put her scarf around her shoulders, and they walked out. When they got to the truck Fredrick opened the door and helped her in as he always does. Monica and Austin were watching and waving. Austin said, "I like him."

Monica said, "Me too."

On the way back to Tasha's, Fredrick told her how much he liked her brother and sister-in-law. They seemed so in love and that is a remarkable thing.

"I want the same thing," he looked at her. Then he asked, "Do you need to stop anywhere before we get to your place?"

"No, I am good, I just want to get home and check on Ms. Diva."

When they got inside Diva was hopping up and down so excited to see them. "Ok girl, let's get you outside," I tell Fredrick, "I will be right back."

He tells me, "We will be right back."

Diva finds a spot right away, and we head back in. I check Diva's bowls, added more water, then I kicked off my shoes and sat down. "That is better." I start to rub my feet. Fredrick sits beside me and says, "Let me do that." I sit back and he puts my feet in his lap, and he starts massaging. "That feels so good."

"Well, I am a trainer, and I know the body very well." He looks at me with that mischievous smile that I just love.

"Do you, now?" I ask him. I make a come-hither motion with my finger. He climbs over me and looks me in the eyes. I say to him, "Show me." We start kissing.

He pulls back, looks at me and ask, "Are you sure Tasha?"

"Yes," I replied, then we start kissing again. I start sliding his jacket off his shoulders. Once that is off, I pull his shirt out of his pants.

He stops me and ask, "Bedroom?"

I point behind me. He put me in his arms and carries me to the bedroom. Once inside, he put me on my feet, so, I am standing beside the bed. We stand there looking at each other. He looks at the one shoulder where the dress has a bow to hold it. He reaches and unties it; the dress falls to the floor. There I stood in my black bra and lacy black thong. He couldn't speak. She was a sight to see standing there.

I pulled his shirt over his head, "You have on too many clothes," I told him. The shirt was tossed onto a chair. Next, I grabbed his belt buckle and unbuckled it. As I drew the zipper down, I looked into his eyes, they were focused on me. His pants dropped to the floor, and he stepped out of them. I looked at his physique, he was in shape, his whole body was muscular. I loved everything I saw, even down to the underwear. They were tight and fitted him like they were made just for him. We moved towards each other at the same time. No words were said, none were needed at this time. We were kissing and touching. Fredrick was thinking he was the luckiest man ever, and I was thinking this is going to be good especially since it had been a while.

Without realizing when it happened, we were on the bed. At first, I was on top, then suddenly, he was on top. Things started to move fast so he put his protection on, and then he started going slow. He didn't want to rush any of it, he wanted it to be special and he had feelings coming at him that were so different from what he'd ever experienced.

I wanted to scream out his name over and over. The things he was doing to my body, I felt like a volcano about to explode. It was like he knew exactly what to do and when to do it. It was like he was reading my mind, and I was loving it.

Just when we both thought it couldn't get any better there was an eruption that blew our minds, and it was an amazing thing. He was breathing hard and so was I. He collapsed right there on top of me, and we laid there holding each other.

Fredrick was at a loss for words, all he knew was that there was nothing better than this.

My body was still pulsating, I could not forget how in tune Fredrick was with my body. He lifted his head and looked at me. I said, "I guess you do know the body."

He laughed and told me, "You are silly, and thank you for the compliment." He kissed me on the neck and drew me closer to him as we tried to calm our breathing. "This was more than I could have ever imagined," he told me. "I need to tell you something and I hope I don't scare you off." He could feel her tense up. "I knew the first time I looked into your eyes that you had my heart Tasha, and I want you to know I love you." You do not have to say it back I just want you to know this is how I feel.

I relaxed and told him, "Thank you for letting me take my time and for not rushing me." He kissed me until I felt dizzy with joy. I thought right now was perfect.

Meanwhile, outside in the parking lot, Bryan was in a rage. It was late and it looked like Tasha's new man was staying the night. "Well, I guess it is about time for me to make my move." He cranked up his car and said, "I will be back Tasha, and then you will come to me."

Chapter 14

I woke up to the smell of food. I looked over and saw that Fredrick wasn't there. I got up and went into the bathroom. When I came back out, he was holding a tray with breakfast on it and a big smile on his face.

"Good morning sleepy head, climb back in, I got you some of my famous eggs, and of course some coffee."

"I have to take care of Diva first."

"Already done it. She has been out, and I put her food and water down. She is good to go. See, look how happy she is on her pillow."

"Thank you!" I got back in bed, and he placed the tray down in front of me. "This looks good," I took a bite of eggs and they tasted good.

"Don't be acting all surprised," he said.

"Well, you said you couldn't cook."

"These are eggs, anyone can fix eggs. And eggs are what I survive on. So, what do you have going on today?" Fredrick asked me.

"I took today off. How about you? I thought you would be gone to work by now."

"I only have a couple of clients today, but I think I might take the day off also. How would you like to hang out together? We could go to Kennesaw Mountain and walk off all that tasty food that your brother fed us last night."

"I would love too; I could use a good workout."

"Great, I am going to run to my place and get myself together and move my clients around. I will call you on my way back."

"Ok," I smiled at him.

While Fredrick was gone, I got myself together then I called the salon. Connie answered, "Betty's Best Look, how may I assist you?"

"Connie, it's Tasha"

"Oh, hi Tasha! Enjoying your day off?"

"Yes, I am, thanks for asking. I'm just calling to see if you booked anyone for tomorrow morning yet?"

"Yes, you have an eleven o' clock already, and the rest of the day is looking good also."

"Ok, I just wanted to check. Thanks Connie!"

"You are welcome, Tasha."

Then I called Ms. Nancy to let her know I would drop Diva off soon. I went to the kitchen and made a green smoothie. I was sipping on that and petting Diva, then my phone starting ringing, it was Alisha.

"Hey girl!" She said as soon as Tasha answered. "You're not working today?"

"No, I took today off."

"You, ok? You sound different. You sound a little perky...wait a minute, you finally got some didn't you?"

Tasha gasped, "How did you know?"

"I know how a woman sounds when she has been pleasured."

"Girl, I just can't, not with you!"

"Ok, spill the beans. How was he?"

"Really, Alisha?! I don't ask you about how Micah was!"

"Because I don't give you a chance too, I just tell you."

"That is so true," I said. We both laughed. "All I am going to say is because he is a trainer he knows his way around a body, ok?"

"Alright then," Alisha said I can tell you are happy, so good for you girl. What did Austin think of your new beau?"

"He likes him."

"Good now it's my turn to check him out."

I say to her, "I am telling you; you will like him. How is Micah? Is everything ok with you guys?"

"Yes, it is a long story, we'll talk about it when you come over. I will tell you this much though, he is a keeper, Tasha."

"What? You are done man hunting? I have got to meet this guy."

"Funny Tasha, very funny."

I finally stopped laughing, "I am happy for you girl. We will talk soon about getting together."

As soon as she clicked off with Alisha, Fredrick called. "Just about there," he said.

"I let him know, I am ready."

Fifteen minutes later, I got a text. "At the door," it read. I opened the door and let him in.

"You ready for a good workout?" He asked me.

"I am, but first we have to drop Diva off at Ms. Nancy's."

"Oh, that reminds me," he reached into his pocket and pulled out a toy for Diva. He bent down and picked her up, then he put the toy to her snout so she could sniff it. She grabbed it and wiggled for him to put her down. So, he put her down, and she went over to her pillow to play with her new toy.

I said, "That was so sweet of you."

"No problem, I am glad she likes it."

"I think she does, but I have to take her to Ms. Nancy's now so she will have to wait to play with it later."

Over at Ms. Nancy's there was a lot of happy barking. "The way they carried on, you would think they hadn't seen each other in months," Ms. Nancy said. "So, what are you young people going to do today?"

"We are going to go walking at Kennesaw Mountain since it is such a lovely day. Pretty soon it will be too cold, so we want to take advantage of it while we can."

"Well, you two have a fun time."

"Thank you," they told her as they left.

"I hope you're ready for a fun day Ms. Tasha."

"Sure, I can't believe you are playing hooky from work to hang out with me."

"I will always do what it takes to hang out with you," he told me as he grabbed my hand."

We arrived at the parking lot, and it was full. Everyone else was taking advantage of the nice day as well. Fredrick finally found a parking spot and pulled in. We got out and Fredrick retrieved his backpack from the trunk.

"What is in the backpack?"

"Just a few provisions we will need, I am like a boy scout. I'm always prepared."

We started out walking at a good pace, stopping to look at something every now and then that caught our eye.

"This was a fantastic idea, I'm enjoying being out here today," I said.

Fredrick asked me if I needed any water.

"No, I am good, we're almost there."

"I'm so glad we could do this today. It's fun to forget about work sometimes and just do what you like, so let us make the most of this day because it is back to work tomorrow."

Not long after that, we reached the top of the mountain. We walked over to the side where the skyline could be seen in the distance. For a moment we stood there looking and not saying anything, just enjoying the view. It wasn't crowded at that time. Fredrick saw a spot to sit down. He grabbed my hand and said, "Let's go sit for a while." He took off the backpack, unzipped it, and pulled out two bottles of water and two sandwiches.

I looked at him and said, "Ok boy scout!"

He smiled at me and said, "Always prepared."

"Well, I'm glad you are because I was getting hungry."

He got out some wet wipes and handed me some.

"Ok I have to ask you, were you a boy scout?"

"I was," he laughed. It was a fun time for me, and I learned a lot.

I unwrapped my sandwich and took a bite. "This is good, where did you get these from?"

"I made them," Fredrick said with a smile.

"There you go, surprising me again. They're just so neatly wrapped, and the sandwich is put together so well, it's like they were professionally done."

"That's because I was making them for someone I happen to care about very much." He leaned in and gave me a kiss on the cheek.

"You are spoiling me."

"I am going to keep on spoiling you. You deserve it."

"Fredrick…"

"Yes," he looked at me.

"Thank you"

"You are welcome. Now let's take some pictures to remember this day he smiled."

We took pictures of each other separately, then selfies. The last one I kissed him, then sent the pictures to him so he could remember the moment. He texted me back, "Best day ever." We held hands as we headed back down the mountain.

Once we got to the truck and got settled, he said to me, "Now it's time for me to take you home so that you can get some rest. I have some things I must take care of. I started working on my website for the home workout business, and I have to get some cards printed out."

"That's great! If you need any help let me know."

"I will, and I appreciate that. Have you been looking for a place for your salon?"

"Just been pricing certain areas. I will seriously start checking out places next year. I'm hoping to have a place open by next year."

"Sounds like you have it all figured out."

"I think so. The hardest part will be leaving the salon I work at now, it's been a wonderful place to work at and learn."

"Look at us, with our plans," Fredrick said.

"These plans are something we are going to make come alive," I told him as we turned into my condo's parking lot. He got out and came to my side of the truck. "We have to go get Diva."

So, we walked over to Ms. Nancy's. I called her in advance to let her know I was coming. As soon as we approached the door, Ms. Nancy opened it.

"Did you two have fun?"

"Yes," we answered. "How was everything here?" I asked as I picked up Diva.

"Well, when we go out Diva acts kind of strange."

"What do you mean by strange?" Fredrick inquired.

"She starts acting like she smells something that is upsetting her. She wines and tries to pull me towards the parking lot. When we come back inside, she is fine. Has she been sick lately?" Ms. Nancy asked Tasha.

"No, she's been well."

Fredrick looked at me but didn't say anything. We were thinking the same thing. Diva is still picking up Bryan's scent, which means he is still coming around.

"Thanks for letting me know Ms. Nancy. I will keep an eye on her and give her some extra love today. Hopefully, that will make her happy."

As they were walking to Tasha's condo, Fredrick was looking around checking out the area. He did not like the feeling he was getting. We got inside and Diva went straight for her new toy.

"He is still coming around, isn't he?" I looked at Fredrick.

Fredrick said, "I believe so." He sat down and pulled me onto his lap. I wrapped my arms around him. He wanted to comfort me, so he began rubbing my back. I never thought someone could care this much.

"It is funny, he brought her for me, but she never liked him. I just don't want Diva stressing. She will not eat, and if that happens, I'll have to take her to the vet. Pomeranians do not do well with stress."

"She seems ok right now," he replied.

"Yes, I am going to make sure she is by spending the rest of the day on this couch with her. We are going to sit here and watch television. So, you go ahead and take care of what you have too. I just need one thing before you go."

"What is that?" Fredrick asked.

"Just give me one of those smiles that you have. There is just something about your smile that makes me so happy."

He started smiling, and I started smiling, and just like that everything was good. He kissed me, and I held onto him as if he was not coming back again.

"Ok, I better get going or I won't be able to tear myself away from you."

I stood up so that he could get up. He walked over to Diva and gave her a rub, then said, "Call me if you need me, I'll check on you later before I go to bed." He pulled me in for another kiss. He gave me a big squeeze and then walked out the door.

Fredrick stood outside until he heard her lock the door and set the alarm. While walking to his truck, he thought about how much he did not want to leave her. He needed to know more about Bryan just in case things went bad for Tasha, and he knew exactly who he had to talk too.

I wanted to ask him to stay but I did not want to seem needy. It was still kind of early even though it was getting dark outside. So, I looked for something to watch on tv; Diva was sitting in my lap. As I was sitting on the couch watching a movie, I was thinking about my sister-in-law, so I picked up my phone and gave her a call.

Monica answered right away, "Tasha how are you?"

I replied, "I am good, how about you little mommy to be?"

"Everything is great, your brother is spoiling me like crazy. He is running me a bath right now. If it were up to him, I wouldn't have to lift a finger. I might try to stay pregnant forever," she laughed.

"You say that now, but I am sure you're going to change your mind about that."

"You might be right," Monica said.

"I just wanted to check up on you."

"That's so sweet, thank you!"

Austin yells, "Annie are you ok?"

"Please tell him I am ok."

"How about you two talk?" Monica handed Austin the phone. "I am going to my bath. Bye, Tasha!"

Austin grabbed the phone, "Hi, Lil sis!"

"Hello dad to be."

"Is Fredrick there?"

"No, he was, but he took off a little while ago."

"You know he is crazy about you right?"

"Yes, he has let me know that."

"So, how about you? How do you feel about him?"

"Why are you trying to be a parent already?"

"I am looking out for my sister."

"Look, I know you are, but understand when I say this- I don't want to say how I feel right now and thank you Austin for always looking out for me. I love you, now go join your wife in the tub."

"Way to change the subject sis, I will go and do just that. Call me if you need me. Love you."

"Love you back." I already knew how I felt about Fredrick, I just didn't want to voice it out loud. I wanted this kept close to my heart. I closed my eyes and thought about his smile. Next thing I knew, I had dozed off to sleep. The sound of I stomach rumbling woke me, so I headed to the kitchen and got a bowl of cereal. My phone started ringing, Fredrick's name showed up I said, "Hello, could you tell I was thinking about you?"

"I hope that means I am very special."

I could just imagine the smile on his face. I asked, "Did you take care of the stuff you had to do?"

"Yes," he answered, "I got everything done. How are things there?"

"All good, I am still on the couch just enjoying being lazy. When I get off the phone with you, I am going to get ready for bed."

"So, you haven't taken Diva out yet?"

"No, not yet. Why?"

"Please, for my peace of mind, can you take her out now with me still on the phone with you."

"Ok, hold on while I hook her up." After hooking the leash on Diva, I picked up the phone and told him, ok heading out now."

"I will sleep better if I know you've already done it, so thank you for humoring me."

"She found a spot." Good girl.

Fredrick asked, "Is she acting normal?"

"Yes, she is fine. We are headed back in." I tell him, "I have locked the door and set the alarm."

He said, "Good, now I can relax some. Did you have a relaxing time today," Fredrick asked her?

"I did and thank you for spending the day with me."

"No problem, I enjoyed it also. I wish I were still there with you now. I want to be with you all the time. Can we talk about where this is going, and please let me know if I am pressuring you because I don't want to do that? I know how I feel, and I have told you. I would love to know how you are feeling."

"Truth be told, I didn't want to have any feeling for anyone, that is why I kept to myself, but I have to say that you came along and opened my heart, and you got in, and I am incredibly happy that you did. You have come to mean a lot to me, Fredrick, and I wish you were here with me too."

"So, I am growing on you?"

"Yes, you are."

"Now I know I will sleep well tonight."

"Why is that?"

"Because, you have let me know that I'm special to you Ms. Tasha, and that has given me hope."

Chapter 15

Friday was a busy day at the salon. Everything went well and there was no drama going on with the ladies and that was a good thing. I left the salon around six thirty, stopped by Chick-fil-A for a salad and nuggets for Diva. When I got home there was a rose outside my door. I picked it up and went inside. I thought to myself, I would call Fredrick later and thank him.

Diva could smell the nuggets and was excited. Ms. Nancy left a note saying she had brought Diva back at five, so I knew Diva didn't have to go out yet.

I changed into something more relaxing, then sat down to eat my salad. I fed Diva a piece of nugget every so often. When I finished, I called Fredrick. I did not want to wait for him to call me like he said he would.

"Hi Tasha, you good?"

"Yes, I just wanted to thank you for the rose I found outside my door when I got home."

"What rose? I did not do that Tasha. I'm on my way over right now." He hung up and didn't even wait for her to respond.

I was holding the phone to my ear and staring at the rose. I jumped up and took the rose to the trash can and threw it in.

Twenty minutes later Fredrick sent me a text, "I am at the door." I opened the door for him then threw myself into his arms.

"I am sorry you came all the way over here for nothing."

"I came for you, Tasha you mean everything to me."

"I came home and saw the rose, I just assumed it was from you. I never thought it could be from Bryan."

"Come, let's sit down," he told her. We headed for the couch. He slid his bag off his shoulder. I looked at it and asked him if he had been at work? "I had just got home, so I threw some stuff in here and came right over. I will not be leaving here tonight, even if I have to stay in my truck." He saw the expression on my face, I was smiling.

"Now I have done it. I've found someone that is more protective than my brother," I laughed. "You don't have to sleep in the truck."

"Good, because I don't want to be uncomfortable sleeping in that truck," he laughed.

"Thanks for the laugh, it's exactly what I needed."

"I am happy that I could make you laugh."

"So have you eaten anything?" I asked him.

"Yes, I ate before I left work, so I'm good. Did you?"

"I picked up something on the way home. I ate it before I called you.

"How about we just try and relax."

We talked about our day and schedules for tomorrow. Fredrick told me he had spoken to his parents recently and they are anxious to meet you.

"Really," I replied with some nervousness in my voice.

"Don't worry, they're going to love you just like I do. Fredrick knew his parents wanted what was best for him, and Tasha was that."

He could tell she cared for him and that was good enough for him right now.

"How about a glass of wine?"

"Sure, that would be nice." While I went to get the wine, he turned on the tv and started channel surfing. I came back and handed him a glass.

"So, what are you watching?"

"Not sure yet, is there anything in particular that you want to see?"

"Not really, keep going. If I see anything interesting, I'll let you know."

He came across a football game and stopped to check it out. "Do you mind?"

"No, go right ahead."

We got comfortable on the couch. Diva was on her pillow sleeping. A commercial came on and I asked him if he played sports in school.

"Yes, I played football in high school, in middle school it was baseball. How about you? Please tell me you were a cheerleader."

"As a matter of fact, I was, and I played softball."

"I would have loved to see you cheer," he said with a big grin on his face.

The game came back on, the other team scored a touchdown and Fredrick turned the channel.

"This game sucks."

A movie was on, someone was getting married. He asked Tasha, "Do you want a big wedding when you get married?"

"I want the whole massive thing because I don't plan on getting married more than once. I want it to be like a fairytale wedding fit for a princess."

He loved the smile she had on her face as she talked about it. Fredrick was loving everything about this whole night, except the rose thing. Being here with her like this was great. He wanted this forever and always. They finished their wine and Tasha took the glasses to the kitchen, then she returned and told him it was time for Diva to go out before bedtime.

"Ok, let's go." Said Fredrick.

It did not take Diva long to find her spot, and they went back inside.

"Good girl Diva," I told her.

I told Fredrick I was going to take a shower. "Help yourself to anything," and I went to my room. He returned to watching the television. After a few minutes, he looked down and there was Diva looking up at him.

"You want to come up here?" She wagged her tail. He took that to mean 'yes,' so he reached down and picked her up. He went back to the game, things had turned around, so he started watching it again. When a commercial came on he would play with Diva. The game ended with his team winning. He turned off the tv just when Tasha was coming out of her room. She was wearing a little black satin robe and heavenly scent that got his attention right away.

"What is that scent you are wearing?"

"Just a Lil body mist from Victoria's Secret."

"You love that place, don't you?"

"I think you were wearing something from there before."

"You remember that?"

"Of course, I remember that." He stood up holding Diva, walked over to her, handed Diva over, grabbed his bag and said, "My turn."

I told him I left a towel set for him on the counter in the bathroom as I watched him walk away. I rinsed the wine glasses and put them in the dishwasher, then began straightening up the couch and turning out lights. I returned to my bedroom and lit a few candles then started pulling the comforter down and throwing pillows on the bench. I had not been happy about the rose on my doorstep, but I was happy about Fredrick showing up on my doorstep. Tasha was still wearing her little robe when he came out of the bathroom, and she was making sure her bag was ready for tomorrow he noticed. He walked out in his boxer briefs; he was one good looking man. Those broad shoulders, abdominal muscles were ripped, biceps that were big, but not too big, and those thighs- now they were muscular.

"I hope you don't mind; I don't do pajamas."

"No, I don't mind at all," I said, while gazing at his body."

He noticed that candles were lit, they gave the room a romantic ambiance. Fredrick looked back at her and saw that the belt on her robe had come unloose and underneath she wore a red bralette and a pair of red lacy panties. He walked towards her, "Is this Victoria's Secret too?"

Looking down, she noticed her robe had come undone, "Yes, it is."

"I am beginning to love that store also, and that color looks so good on you." He held out his hands to me, I put my hands in his, he looked at me and smiled. He led me to the bed, we both sat down on the edge facing each other. He began trailing kisses on my neck. The smell of his cologne wrapped around my body. I could also feel my heartbeat faster. Fredrick had a way of making that happen to me. Just being near him did things to me. I had to admit I was loving it; I drew myself up closer to him. The next thing Fredrick knew, I took over and he had no objections. He decided to let me have my way. Who would have guessed that she would go all in for hers? When it was all finished and we were just holding one another, Fredrick told

me, "Girl, you just wore me out, and I just want to say thank you."
We both laughed.

"I think I wore myself out too," I yawned, I got up and walked
to the bathroom. When I came out, he went in. I blew out the candles
and got back in bed. I turned to my side, a few minutes later, I felt
him get into the bed. He got close behind me and kissed me on my
back, then said, "Goodnight."

"Goodnight," I replied.

Chapter 16

The next morning, I got up before him and made smoothies. He came in a few minutes later all dressed his bag on his shoulder.

"Morning. You got up early."

"Well, I slept good last night."

He walked over to me and gave me a kiss. "Sorry, but I have to get going. I have a client this morning. How about I bring some food later after work?"

"That sounds good. I should be home around four today since it is Saturday.

"Alright, I will see you around six."

"Would you like a smoothie to go?

"I will take one. Thanks, I'll drink it on the way to the gym, and I have some protein bars in the truck also."

"I poured the smoothie and handed it to him. Have a great day," she sent him off with a kiss.

I got to work and was humming to myself as I was getting my workstation ready for the day. My co-workers were looking at me smiling. Ms. Betty walked over and said, "Got some last night didn't you."

I looked at her and said, "I don't kiss and tell Ms. Betty and I continued getting ready.

"Well, you don't have to, we," and she waved her hand around to indicate, "The rest of the ladies can tell that you did."

I looked around to see the other ladies looking at me and smiling.

"So, is it the same guy that sent you the roses?"

"Kiss and tell Ms. Betty, kiss and tell."

Connie came over and told Tasha her client had arrived. Tasha smiled at Ms. Betty and went to greet her client.

Halfway through her day Tasha got a text from Fredrick that said, "I am still thinking about last night." With a smile emoji.

Blushing, I replied with a smiley emoji. Yes, I was loving this, having someone in my life that made me smile and treated me well. I had a light lunch to save room for whatever Fredrick was planning to bring over. I was so happy, and it had been a while since I had been. Tomorrow we were going to Alisha's which will prove to be very entertaining. Work should wrap up around three, giving me plenty of time to get home and get ready.

My last two clients arrived late; it never fails. It was raining and traffic was terrible, thank goodness it was just haircuts. I worked diligently and got them done. I was headed out the back door when I saw Ms. Betty was in the back getting ready to leave also. I stood at the door, "Ms. Betty his name is Fredrick."

Ms. Betty smiled, "I am happy for you Tasha."

"Goodnight," I replied with a smile.

It took me an extra twenty minutes to get home. When I arrived, Diva was at the door happy to see me. The note said she had just got home around three thirty, so she didn't have to worry about taking Diva out, since it was only five. I put on a pair of sweatpants and a pullover hoodie. My phone buzzed; it was Fredrick. I went to the door to let him in.

"Hello beautiful," he stepped inside and handed me a bag of food and shut the door behind himself. Diva was excited because she could smell the food. Fredrick laughed at her behavior. We went to

112

the kitchen, "I stop by an Italian restaurant and bought two different dishes- hope that is ok with you?"

"I'm sure there is something in here I'll love." I took the food out of the bag and put it on the counter. He brought pasta with chicken and Alfredo sauce, stuffed chicken marsala, and of course some bread. "This looks good. What do you want to drink?"

"Do you have some tea"

"Yes, can you grab it out of the fridge."

"Sure," he went to the sink and washed his hands. I got the plates and the glasses. He grabbed the tea and silver ware and we sat down and started filling our plates.

Fredrick asked if I had heard from my brother lately?

"I called to check on Monica and we talked for a while.

"Monica good?"

"Yes, she is doing well."

"That's good to hear."

Diva was whining so Tasha gave her a piece of chicken.

"Is it ok for her to have that?" He asked.

"It's fine, I don't do it a lot. So, are you ready for Alisha's place tomorrow?"

"I'm ready to meet your bestie."

"Just remember she's my crazy friend."

"If you call her a friend then she's a good person because I know you wouldn't hang with her if you didn't think she was."

"You are so right. I have not met her boyfriend yet. All I know is she's crazy about him."

"Do she want us to bring anything?"

"No, she said just bring ourselves."

We finished our meals, and afterwards put the food and dishes away. I liked that he knew his way around my place.

"So how was everything when you got home today?"

I looked at him puzzled by his question. I pondered over it for a few seconds, then I realized he was making sure there were no more surprises for me when I got home. "Things were good, no problems."

"Good, did you tell your brother about yesterday?"

"Are you kidding? He would have me packed up and moved in with him already. I won't tell him anything." I walked over to him and wrapped my arms around him. We stood there for a while hugging each other. "So, tell me Fredrick, where are you staying tonight?"

"That depends," he said, "Are you asking me to stay?"

I pulled back and looked at him, "Yes, I am asking."

"Then I'm staying. So, it is still kind of early. What do you want to do?"

"Well, I need to go to the pet store. Diva needs some dog food."

"Ok, my chariot waits for my two princesses."

"That is funny," I told him.

I went to get my cardigan sweater and a pair of rain boots. I put Diva's leash on, "Oh, do you mind if she rides in your truck?"

"No, I don't mind."

The pet store wasn't too far away. When we got to the store all the workers were saying hello to Diva.

Fredrick said, "How much time do you spend in this store?"

"Not a lot," I said with a grin. "This is just how it is with Ms. Diva; I only take her to a few places where she is well known. She isn't called Diva for nothing."

We walked to the dog food isle, "Which one?" He asked me.

"This one," I pointed. He picked up the bag and we headed back to the front of the store.

"Anything else?"

"No, that's it."

On the way back home Fredrick said, "She really is your baby, isn't she?"

"Yes," Diva was sitting on Tasha's lap looking at him as if to say, 'Do you even have to ask?'

With that done and Diva all set for the night, we settled on the couch to watch a movie. I popped popcorn, fixed drinks, and we were happy as could be. To Fredrick this was it. There wasn't any place else he would rather be on a cold, rainy night. He was in her little world, and he intended to stay.

Chapter 17

We woke up that Sunday morning, had breakfast and coffee, then he left for work. All day long I thought about Fredrick and how I was missing him.

Fredrick was at work trying his best to concentrate, but it proved difficult. All he could think about was Tasha. People kept asking if he was feeling, ok? He was so in love with Tasha he just had to make sure she did not get away. I made it through the day. I went to church and then back home.

Ms. Nancy still had Diva. She said she would bring her back later. I was feeling so relaxed I almost fell asleep. I looked at the time and jumped up, I had to start getting ready. My outfit laid on the bed, ready for me to put on after I got out of the shower.

After getting dressed, my phone buzzed. It was Fredrick. I opened the door and there he was, looking very handsome. He walked in and waited for her to close the door, then gave her a big hug. Fredrick was wearing jeans with a sweater, and a pair of black boots.

"You look good," I told him.

"So do you in those jeans, and those boots are very sexy on you."

I smiled, "Thank you," I said as I grabbed my short black leather jacket and slid it on.

"Where is my other girl?"

"She's with Ms. Nancy still hanging out with Buster. You ready to have some crazy fun?"

"Yes, let's go have some fun."

Alisha lived about thirty minutes away from Tasha. She had family that worked in real estate, and they helped her find the house some years back. Alisha had worked hard to fix it up. We pulled up in front of a house that had a cozy look to it. Fredrick parked, stepped out, and walked to the passenger side to let Tasha out. We got to the door and rung the bell. It opened and there stood a tall muscular, good-looking guy who looked like he could be a bodyguard.

"You must be Tasha and Fredrick. Come on in, I'm Micah," he extended his hand out to Fredrick.

I noticed his deep voice, that was check one Alisha.

"Nice to finally meet you, Tasha! Alisha talks about you all the time. She's in the kitchen, I'll take you to her."

I had eyes on him as he walked us to the kitchen. Muscles, I thought, check two Alisha. I was about to say, 'something smells good,' when I spotted Alisha talking something out of the fridge. "Girl, you got it smelling good up in here."

"I've been slaving away in this kitchen." We gave each other a hug.

"Alisha this is Fredrick, remember girl no crazy I whispered."

Alisha gives Tasha the biggest smile ever and held out her hand, "Hi, Fredrick! It's so nice to meet you." She looks over at Tasha with an 'I *can* be nice face.'

Fredrick smiles at them both. "Nice to meet you also."

Alisha walks over and stands by Micah who has a smile on his face as well. "So, everyone has been introduced, right?" Alisha asked. "Great! What can I get you to drink?"

"Wine for me," Tasha tells her.

"Me also," Fredrick replied.

Micah chose wine too.

"I'll help you," Tasha said.

"Thanks, Tasha. Ok, why don't you fellas make yourselves comfortable. We'll join you in a few."

Micah told her, "Ok, but don't talk about us for too long." He and Fredrick walked away laughing.

That is check three, Tasha thought. Alisha and I looked at each other and started giggling like schoolgirls.

"So, girl, Micah seems to be all of the fantasy men you wanted rolled into one."

"I told you, he's a keeper. Now Fredrick, that smile is something else."

"Yes, that's what got me. All he has to do is smile and everything in my world is ok."

They finished pouring the drinks. "You think they're talking about us too?" I asked Alisha.

"Could be." As they carried the drinks out of the kitchen. I asked her, "What did you find out about Micah? You know the gut feeling?"

"Oh, he has a daughter, and he thought I wouldn't be happy about that."

"How do you feel about it?"

"Well, she's three years old, so she's with her mom most of the time. He tries to spend a lot of time with her. I've met her, she's so precious."

"What about the mom?"

"They're on good terms. She's married now, so all is well."

"I don't know what to say. I am shocked. You and a kid!"

"I know right? I didn't see that one coming." They join up with the guys chilling in the living room.

118

"My ears are on fire, how about yours Fredrick," Micah asks?

"Micah, you know you are my favorite subject to talk about, so stop trying to be funny," Alisha said.

Fredrick slid over so Tasha could sit beside him. She handed him his wine.

"So, what are you guys talking about?" Alisha asked.

"Sports of course, that is what we do."

"Well, time to change the subject. I'm so glad that we could get together, it's time we all get to know each other," Alisha said looking at Fredrick.

"Here we go," thought Tasha.

"What would you like to know?" He looks at Alisha.

"Well, I know you're a trainer, and I know how you two met. You know what she's been through." Fredrick nods, listening intently and waiting for the big question.

"So, I want to know what your intentions are towards my best friend?"

"Really, Alisha?" You are worse than Austin.

Alisha puts her hand up at Tasha as to say stay out of this.

"It's ok Tasha," Fredrick told her. He looked at Alisha and gave her his most charming smile. He says "I intend to be in her life for as long as she will allow, to love her for as long as she will have me, and to protect her from anything bad that comes her way. I have told her, and I'll tell you because I know how close you two are. I love her," then he looked at Tasha. She took his hand and held on to it.

Alisha looked at them both and saw it- her best friend was happy, and Alisha had not seen that in a long time.

"Anything else?" Fredrick asked her.

Alisha said, "No, I believe you have taken care of my curiosity. Thank you."

"You are welcome." Fredrick said.

"Now let's relax and have some fun." Alisha smiled.

They were talking and enjoying themselves when Alisha informed them dinner was ready, so they headed to the dining room. The room was painted dark grey, since there were such large windows in the room it received ample natural lighting, so there was never an issue of it being too dark. The trim was a light grey, and there was a light grey table with four chairs. The table was set up beautifully. There was a tall candelabra in one corner with a lot of candles on it. In another corner stood a huge palm plant. Up against another wall was a long mirror, and on the other wall was long table with a lamp on it. There were crystal balls hanging from the lamp. Candles in different heights and a round tray with crystal glasses and a crystal decanter sitting upon it.

"Please take a seat," Alisha told everyone, "And excuse me, I am going to get the food."

"I will help you," Tasha volunteered.

"More girl talk," Micah said, with a smile on his face. When they left Micah told Fredrick, "Man, I apologies for Alisha giving you the third degree. As you can tell, she's protective of Tasha.

"It's all good," Fredrick said, "I'm glad she has a good friend, and Tasha warned me about her already."

"Alisha's a handful and some more, but she has a good heart and I like that about her."

The ladies came back carrying plates. Tasha put one down for Fredrick and the other for herself. Alisha placed one down for Micah, then her own. The wine was already on the table.

"This looks so good!" Tasha said. "Thank you for going through all this trouble."

"No trouble at all, and you are welcome."

There was filet mignon with three grilled shrimp on top, covered in a buttery garlic sauce. A twice baked potato with brussels sprouts along with a basket of butter rolls.

Micah picked up his glass and said, "To the cook." Everyone toasted.

"So, Micah, your turn. How do you put up with Alisha?" Tasha asked him with a smirk on her face.

Alisha got ready to defend herself, until Tasha put her hand up to stop her, just as Alisha had done to her before when questioning Fredrick. Everyone else laughed, and Alisha closed her mouth in defeat.

Once Micah stopped laughing, he looked at Fredrick and said, "I hope I answer this question as well as you did yours." Then he said to Tasha, "The more I get to know Alisha, the more I fall for her. She has this wall of toughness that she puts up, but I know behind that wall she's the sweetest lady I know and, I think I have found my queen."

Alisha eyes lit up; everyone could tell she was happy with that answer.

I heard my phone ringing from the other room, so I excused myself to answer it. I pulled it out of my bag, it was Ms. Nancy.

Ms. Nancy blurted out, "I took the doggies out and was going to drop off Diva, but out of nowhere this man ran up, snatched Diva and took off. Tasha, it looked like Bryan."

I burst into tears and started saying," No, no, no," over and over. I told her," I am on my way," and hung up.

Fredrick heard her and came in with Alisha and Micah trailing behind him. "What is wrong?"

Tasha put her hand over her mouth and ran to the bathroom and threw up what little food she just ate.

121

"Tasha, what happened?"

"Diva, he took my Diva!" And she began crying hysterically.

Fredrick pulled her to him trying to comfort her, but it was not working. He motioned for Alisha to come over and get her. Alisha headed to the bedroom with Tasha.

"I'll be back, please take care of her and don't let her leave," said Fredrick.

"Where are you going?" Asked Alisha.

"I am going to get Diva back."

"Do you even know what Bryan looks like?"

"I know everything I need to know about Bryan."

"Micah, you better go with him. He looks like he's going to kill Bryan if he finds him."

"You're right." He took off behind Fredrick.

"Please be careful!" Alisha yelled at them.

Chapter 18

As Fredrick was driving through the streets wide open, he called Austin. Austin answered, "Fredrick, how are you?"

"Not so good man, we got a problem," he told Austin what happened.

"Where are you now Austin asked him?"

"I'm just about at a house that I know he hangs out at?" Fredrick told him the address.

"Ok, I am calling the cops and I am on the way. I pray the cops get there before I do." He hung up.

Micah said, "Alisha told me about this Bryan guy, he needs his ass kicked."

"Don't worry," Fredrick said, "He's about to get that."

They pulled up in front of the house. They both got out of the truck and ran up to the door. Someone was just coming out, so they pushed their way inside. Fredrick looked around for Bryan, he did not see him, but he heard a bark from inside a room down the hallway, and there was the sound of a bottle hitting a wall and shattering. Fredrick burst through the door; Micah was right behind him. There was Bryan sitting there looking like he was out of it. Diva was hiding under a table. Fredrick told Micah to close the door. He went over to Bryan, grabbed him by the collar and he didn't say one word, he just started punched him like he was a punching bag. You could hear the sirens become louder as the cops approached. Micah had to pull Fredrick off Bryan.

123

"You're going to kill him if you don't stop, and he won't be the only one going to jail."

Fredrick stopped and walked away to calm down. He knew Diva was scared so he had to get himself together to get her to come to him. Micah was keeping an eye on Bryan to make sure he didn't try anything. They could hear the cops rummaging through the house. Micah looked down and saw a white, fluffy dog walking toward Fredrick very slowly. He said, "Look down." Fredrick did, Diva had come to him, and she was wagging her tail. He reached down and picked her up. She licked his hand in thanks. Fredrick could hear his name being called, the door opened, it was Austin.

"You, ok?" He asked Fredrick.

"Yeah, can't say the same for him though."

Austin looked over towards Bryan. He wanted to beat him some more, but Micah saw the look in his eyes and stopped him.

"No need to, man. He is half dead. Your guy here put a good whipping on him."

Austin looked up at him, then to Fredrick. "Who is the muscle?"

Fredrick smiled, "This is Micah, he's Alisha's muscle."

Austin looked him up and down and said, "Alisha?" He put out a hand, Micah shook it. Austin told him, "Good luck with that." They all laughed.

The cops came in. The medics were called, and Bryan was looked over and put on a stretcher. After Austin talked to the cops, they handcuffed him to it.

"Where is my sister?" Ask Austin.

"She's with Alisha at her house."

"Let's go, I want to check on her."

Diva barked; Austin rubbed her on the head. "Glad you are ok, girl."

In the truck, Diva would not leave Fredrick's lap. Austin was following them over to Alisha's. He called Ms. Nancy on the way and told her that they found Diva, and she was safe and, on her way, back to Tasha.

Ms. Nancy was in tears, thanking the good Lord. "Did you get Bryan?"

"Yes, he'll get locked up this time. I will make sure of it, but first he'll stay in the hospital. Fredrick beat the crap out of him."

"I like that young man!" Ms. Nancy said.

"Me too, Ms. Nancy."

"Thanks for the call, Austin!"

"You're welcome!"

They arrived at Alisha's. Tasha had cried herself to sleep.

"Hi, Austin."

"Hello Alisha" replied Austin.

Fredrick headed to the room Tasha was in. She was laying on her side facing the other way, so he walked in and called her name."

She didn't move. He sat on the bed, and she moved a little. He placed Diva next to her, so that Diva could lick her face. Tasha sat up on the bed, pulled Diva close to her, and began crying again, this time tears of happiness. She looked at Fredrick, wrapped her other arm around him, saying, "Thank you," she said repeatedly.

Austin knocked on the door to let them know he was there. "I just wanted to make sure you were ok Annie."

She was crying and laughing at the same time. "Yes, I am so happy right now."

"Good, because that it all I want for you Tasha."

"I know," she said, "But what are you doing here?"

"I called him," Fredrick said. "I knew he could help me."

She looked from one to the other as if they had a secret.

"Where is Bryan?" She asked them.

"After Fredrick beat him badly, the cops showed up and took him away," Micah said from the doorway.

"Why did he take Diva?"

The guys were looking like they did not know. Alisha told them he texted Tasha's phone saying he had Diva and if she wanted her back, she had to come and get her.

"So that was his plan," Austin said. "Too bad Fredrick got to him first. They had to get a stretcher for that fool. That is how bad Fredrick beat him.

Tasha looked at Fredrick and started crying again. "Why are you crying again?" He asked her.

"Because I got Diva back and I realized something. I am so happy, and that's because of you. I love you. I have been too afraid to admit it but, I do. You have been so good to me and so patient."

Fredrick said, "I have been waiting to hear you say how you feel." He hugged her and told her he loved her too.

"Let's go home," Tasha said.

Chapter 19

Tasha and Fredrick were inseparable after that. Things were going great, he told her he wanted her to come over to his place for dinner. "How about tomorrow?" Which was going to be Monday.

"Really, you will cook for me?" She said with a smile. "The main question is, can you cook?" She wanted to tease him like he did her when she first cooked for him.

He put his hand over his heart and said, "My feelings are hurt." He gave her a kiss, "I have to go, I have a lot to do, so this is goodnight. Come over around five."

Tasha got up feeling happy. She went and did errands, then went back home and took Diva for a good long walk. Her Mani and Pedi was done earlier. I needed to look and feel my best. A long hot bubble bath was next. She pulled out a sweater dress that hanged off one shoulder. Paired it with over the knee boots. Then she pulled her hair up to show off a pair of chandelier earrings, and she was set.

Diva had everything she needed while Tasha was out. She would sleep off the long walk the entire time Tasha would be gone.

It only took her twenty minutes to get to Fredrick's place. I walked to his door and knocked. The door opened, and there he was. "Hi," he said.

"Hi, yourself," I told him.

"Come on in."

She walked inside and said, "Oh my, this is beautiful." His loft was very spacious. There was this white fabric that had a shear look, set up with lights hanging down. The rest of the loft was blocked off from view. Candles were lit everywhere.

She looked at him, "What's going on?"

He took her coat and hung it up. He then takes her by the hands and looks deeply into her eyes. "Tasha Williams, ever since I have met you, I can't stop thinking about you. And when we are together it hurts me to leave you. I know with all my heart that you were born to be my wife, so I am asking you, would you please be my wife?"

He takes out a small box from his pocket and opens it, showing her the ring. Tears are running down her face. She looks at the ring, then back at him, then says, "Yes, I will."

Fredrick slides the ring on, and from behind the fabric are the sounds of cheering. Out walks Austin and Monica, Alisha and Micah, Ms. Nancy, and a couple Tasha did not know. If she had to guess, they were his parents. He called them over and introduced them to her.

The evening turned out to be so much fun. Austin had someone come over and cook. There was a table set up for nine people. The food was delicious, and the people made everything even better. Tasha and Fredrick held onto each other the rest of the night.

She asked him, "When did you pull all this off and how?"

"Well, I called your brother first to ask for your hand in marriage, then I told him what I had in mind. So, he got the food part taken care of, then I got Alisha to decorate the place. I got my parents to come here, and everything else fell into place. My parents love you already, I told you they would. We're going to have a great life together, I love you, Tasha."

"I love you, Fredrick."

Epilogue

Tasha and Fredrick were married two months later. Fredrick wanted her to have the winter wedding she said she wanted. It was a lot of quick work, but with Alisha's help, they pulled it off. The wedding was held at Austin's house with just family and a few friends. Tasha made sure her salon coworkers were there.

Three months after they married, Fredrick's business grew so much he had to hire employees to help him. Tasha opened her own salon, she called it 'Tasha's Touch.' Ms. Nancy was waiting on a baby to take care of, but that would have to wait a while, they told her. Austin and Monica were still waiting on the arrival of their son.

Alisha and Micah were next to tie the knot. She finally got the man she wanted. And Ms. Diva, well she is still, and will always be, *Ms. Diva*

Coming soon

<u>To Love Again</u>

Carter went into the daycare; it was a busy time of the day when the kids were being picked up. He got to the window outside of Angel's room, there were about four babies left. Angel was playing peek a boo with Raina. Angel was laughing so hard Carter could not help but laugh at her. He absolutely loved it when Angel was happy.

Mrs. Anna saw him and went outside to stand at the window also.

"I see everything is going good," Carter said to her.

"Yes, it has been a fantastic day. She is adapting very well, and the babies love her. Angel has become especially taken with her."

"Really?" Carter said. He looked at Raina, she seemed to be having just as much fun as Angel was having.

"Well, let us see if we can break these two up," Mrs. Anna said with a smile.

As soon as they walked into the room Angel saw Carter she stood up and started wobbling towards him with a smile on her face. He bent down and held out his arms to her.

Raina stood up and watched them. Angel walked right into his arms, he kissed her on the cheek, then she kissed him back.

Raina was thinking you could just see the love between the two of them. She got Angel's bag, then she went over to greet him.

"Hi, how was your day?" she asked him.

"Hello. It was a good day, thank you for asking. How about yours?" He saw Mrs. Anna moving away from them.

"It was the best!" she told him with a big smile. At that time Angel reached down towards her, Carter leaned towards Raina, and she reached for Angel. She put Angel on her hip. Raina told Carter that Angel had a fun day, which is written in her report, inside of her bag. He reached over and took the bag off her shoulder.

"She's a good baby." Raina says with a smile.

Angel was looking at Raina like she understood every word.

Carter told her thank you.

"You are welcome."

Angel did something that shocked them both she gave Raina a kiss on the cheek then she reached for her dad.

They both just stood there looking at each other.

"She likes you Carter told her."

"Well, that's good because I like her too."

About the author

SGerald lives in Hiram, Ga. She has a son and a daughter. One of her favorite things to do is to go out walking with her Pomeranian. When she isn't doing that, reading or writing is how she spends her time.

You may write to me at SGerald@gmail.com

Made in the USA
Columbia, SC
06 January 2022